29 DEC 2012

− 2 MAR 2013

PETERBOROUGH LIBRARIES

~~24 Hour renewal line 08458 505606~~

This book is to be returned on or before the latest date shown above, but may be renewed up to three times if the book is not in demand. Ask at your local library for details.

Please note that charges are made on overdue books

60000 0000 72733

Also by Guy Adams and available from Titan Books:

Sherlock Holmes: The Breath of God

COMING SOON:
Deadbeat: Makes You Stronger

SHERLOCK HOLMES

The Army of Dr Moreau

GUY ADAMS

TITAN BOOKS

Sherlock Holmes: The Army of Dr Moreau
Print edition ISBN: 9780857689337
E-book edition ISBN: 9780857689344

Published by Titan Books
A division of Titan Publishing Group Ltd
144 Southwark Street, London SE1 0UP

First edition: July 2012
10 9 8 7 6 5 4 3 2 1

Names, places and incidents are either products of the author's imagination or are used fictitiously. Any resemblance to actual persons, living or dead (except for satirical purposes), is entirely coincidental.

Guy Adams asserts the moral right to be identified as the author of this work. Copyright © 2012 by Guy Adams.

No part of this publication may be reproduced, stored in a retrieval system, or transmitted, in any form or by any means without the prior written permission of the publisher, nor be otherwise circulated in any form of binding or cover other than that in which it is published and without a similar condition being imposed on the subsequent purchaser.

A CIP catalogue record for this title is available from the British Library.

Printed and bound in the USA.

What did you think of this book? We love to hear from our readers. Please email us at: readerfeedback@titanemail.com, or write to us at the above address.

To receive advance information, news, competitions, and exclusive offers online, please sign up for the Titan newsletter on our website **www.titanbooks.com**

To James Goss, who will wash it down with cava and cat hair.

**Peterborough
City Council**

60000 0000 72733

Askews & Holts	Aug-2012
CRI	£7.99

"Children of the Law," I said, "(Moreau) is not dead... He has changed his shape—he has changed his body... For a time you will not see him. He is... there —" I pointed upward "—where he can watch you. You cannot see him. But he can see you. Fear the Law."

Edward Prendick in *The Island of Dr Moreau*, H.G. Wells

PART ONE

A Mystery in Rotherhithe

CHAPTER ONE

Writers are surrounded by editors. If there is one thing I have learned in my time working on these stories, it is that.

I have always tried to be an honest chronicler, adhering to the facts wherever legally and morally possible. I've shuffled things around, presented events in the most dramatic order, clarified dialogue and trimmed the wandering up and down flower beds and gravel driveways to a bare minimum. These reports are intended to be exciting after all, and my editor at *The Strand* will soon tell me if I run the risk of boring his readers to death.

Editors, you see? They always want to steer the ship, no matter whose hand is on the tiller.

And what of Holmes? Certainly, he's never slow in offering his opinion. "You are a genius, Watson," he announced only the other day. "To be able to remove every aspect of interest from a case so fascinating as that of the Hamilton Cannibals is astonishing. Every deduction, every piece of analysis – all sacrificed to scenes of you swooning over Lady Clara and chasing around Kent with your service revolver. Perhaps it's time these tales were renamed? Could the reading public finally be ready for *The Tales of John Watson: The Crime Doctor*?"

Of course I could claim near-immunity to Holmes' comments, he makes them so often and with such relish that I take them as little more than bitter seasoning during our mealtime conversations. It amuses him to mock the stories, for they are singularly responsible for the public image he now labours under, an image he would dispel given the slightest chance. Holmes, though in possession of a gargantuan sense of self-importance, never will take to life as a public hero. It implies a morality on him he has no wish to bear.

Then there are the editors in their thousands: the readers.

No, I will qualify that – before I alienate every pair of hands to pick up a copy of *The Strand* – *certain* readers who appear to possess altogether too much spare time. These are the people who write to complain about inaccuracies and inconsistencies. The people who claim to know better. According to these folk I should pass on my pen to another. Perhaps one better able to remember where he was wounded in Afghanistan (the leg *and* the shoulder, thank you Mr Haywood of Leeds), or even what his first name is (my wife often used to call me James, Mrs Ashburton of Colchester, initially mimicking a particularly forgetful client and then simply because the name stuck. She also used to call me Jock, Wattles and Badger, though you can rest assured I shall have no call to repeat the fact now she has passed).

I must confess these are the editors I work hard to ignore. While I will always appreciate the popularity of my work (anyone who says he doesn't care whether people like his writing is a liar), you can never please all of the readers all of the time. Whenever I try to do so, my writing suffers as a consequence.

There will always be those who insist certain stories are fakes, written by other authors attempting to pass off what Holmes would laugh to hear me refer to as my "style", or those who complain that the contents are unbelievable. The latter will be particularly vocal when – or perhaps I should say *if* – our last case, the curious affair I have titled "The Breath of God", comes to print. There's nothing that a certain band of readers likes less than ambiguity, a quality that adventure certainly possessed. Conversely there are many who rate such fantastical adventures higher than those grounded in reality. The public's appetite for the bizarre will always be considerable. Which is why I can never resist selecting such cases, even though I know that many of them will join the considerable stack of writing I have completed that will never see print in my lifetime.

The affair that immediately followed that of The Breath of God, the complex business I turn my attention to now, will be yet another forced to gather dust rather than readers. It will also stretch the credulity of that unhappy band of readers who demand that everything keep to the well-worn and easily believed. That this was to be the case was obvious from the first, for certainly nothing ever came from Mycroft Holmes that was conventional.

Mycroft Holmes appears rarely in my written accounts – no doubt that critical band of my readership can remind me precisely how often. This is not because he was a stranger to his younger brother, rather that the cases he involved us in were usually so secret that there was little point in my making any record of them. That could be argued as the case now, though I will gamble the possibility of a few wasted hours in the hope that one day the adventure can see the light of day. As bizarre and horrific, as politically charged and embarrassing to certain members of hallowed governmental offices as it may be, it would be a shame indeed were nobody ever to know the truth with regards to the army of Dr Moreau.

CHAPTER TWO

"Well," announced Holmes, "either the country is on the brink of disaster or word of Mrs Hudson's kedgeree has spread to Mayfair." From his position, cross-legged on the floor before the fire, he raised his head above the parapet of his tobacco-stained nest, a temporary blemish on the carpet built from newspaper personal columns and that morning's mail, and pointed towards the window. "Unless I'm mistaken…"

"Which you never are."

Holmes smiled. "…Mycroft approaches."

The doorbell rang.

"You'll be telling me you could smell his hair wax half a mile away," I joked.

"No," Holmes admitted, "at least," he smiled, "not with the windows closed. Though I can recognise the sound of his tread easily enough and there are few men in London who can make a cab creak with such relief when they offload themselves from it."

I heard the front door open followed by the groan of our stairs.

"Not to mention the agony of our floorboards." We laughed as the door crashed open and the considerable bulk of Mycroft Holmes appeared breathlessly in the doorway.

"Only poor people chose to live in upstairs rooms," he complained. "Kindly have the decency to live up to your bank balance and buy a damned house."

"Then how would you get your bi-annual exercise?"

"Exercise? I have evolved beyond exercise. Only those without a brain would choose to obsess on the flesh. It's a vehicle, nothing more."

Words I'd heard Holmes himself use, though I chose not to mention the fact. "A vehicle that is in need of upkeep, Mycroft," I said. "When was the last time you had a check-up? You're breathing like a bulldog with a bullet wound."

"Dear Lord!" Mycroft shouted, dropping into an unfortunate armchair. "Since when did a gentleman have to endure such slights against his person?"

"When there is so much of his person to slight," Holmes replied and erupted into laughter, throwing the remnants of his morning correspondence, fluttering, into the air.

"Oh no," Mycroft said, looking at me, "he's positively effervescent! What's wrong with him?"

"I rather imagine," I replied, "that he is excited by the possibility of work you bring. We've just finished a particularly complex and unusual case and the idea of being able to sink his teeth immediately into a new one…"

"One man's meat is another's poison," Mycroft said, glowering at his brother. "What brings you excitement threatens to breed another ulcer in this stomach that so fascinates you both."

"Another ulcer?" I sighed and fetched my medical bag. If Mycroft wouldn't go and see a doctor I'd force a medical opinion on him while he was too exhausted to move.

"Oh don't fuss!" he said as I advanced upon him. But he knew better than to actually fight me off and I proceeded to conduct a basic examination while Holmes called down for coffee.

"Your heart sounds like a drunken bare-knuckle fight and your blood pressure would see the sleeper train to Glasgow and back. You need to look after yourself. Otherwise, sooner or later, one or the other will kill you."

"Obviously, Doctor," he replied. "Luckily my job is extremely relaxing."

"I shall prescribe you a medical diet and an exercise regimen."

"And I shall have you shot as an enemy of the Crown."

"Follow my advice or end up in an early grave, the choice is yours."

"Coffee," Mrs Hudson announced, bringing in a tray, with a disapproving look on her face. It was a familiar countenance, as much a part of the Baker Street furnishings as the tobacco slipper and the shrunken head that Holmes used as a stopper on a flask of gunpowder. The decoration in those rooms was always wont to make a lady despair.

Mycroft made a childish show of taking a biscuit from the saucer Mrs Hudson had provided and popping it, whole, into his mouth.

"Might we now move onto matters of more importance than my weight?" he asked once he had swallowed. "As much as your concern is gratifying I did not make this arduous journey simply to gossip like an old lady at a bandstand."

"We never get the benefit of your company unless the empire itself is in peril," agreed Holmes. "What is it this time? Treasury lost the keys to the vault?" He paused for effect. "Again?"

He released himself from the clutter of that morning's mail and walked over to the fireplace to refresh his pipe. Holmes knew well enough that a period of contemplation lay ahead and for him, contemplation was impossible without tobacco.

"Gentlemen," Mycroft announced, somewhat theatrically, "what do you know of natural selection?"

"Survival of the fittest," I replied. "The belief that a species adapts according to its environment, Darwinism."

"In a nutshell, Doctor. Though we've come a long way since Darwin's initial writings."

"And who might you mean when you say 'we'?" Holmes asked.

Mycroft shuffled in his chair, something the piece of furniture was lucky to survive. "You are, I assume, suggesting this to be a Departmental affair." The capital "D" was clearly emphasised.

"Naturally, if only to watch you squirm. Need I reassure you of Watson's discretion?"

"I would hope not," I interrupted. After all, given the work I had performed alongside my friend in the name and interest of Queen and country one begins to hope one's reputation can be taken for granted.

"No," Mycroft agreed, "I appreciate you know when to discuss your adventures with my brother and when to keep your notebook locked within the desk." A point that I shall, in haste, gloss over.

"Nonetheless," he continued, "beyond a handful of individuals nobody is supposed to know of the existence of The Department. As you know, I have often been in service to the government, applying such skills as I might possess in the furtherance of the national interest. It was only a matter of time before my role was expanded. While my experience and knowledge is suitably wide there will always be the need for more expert services and that is where The Department comes in, a movable list of agents hired – often without their direct knowledge – in order to handle specific threats or research projects. I am the Headmaster as it were, supervising and selecting those needed and acting as the central focus of the network."

"A central focus in government," said Holmes. "What will they think of next?"

"I cannot deny that the lack of inter-departmental squabbling and compromise of purpose is refreshing," he agreed. "In fact it was a deciding factor when it came to my accepting the post. I operate outside the changing tide of policy and opinion, I do as I see fit. Pursuing the matters that seem to me to be of the most importance."

"And that included evolutionary theory?" I asked.

"Naturally. Whenever a grand shift in scientific thinking comes along it is always the duty of government to lend its attention. You can be sure that other governments are doing the same. Survival of the fittest, Dr Watson, just think of the possible extensions of that thought. Is this a force of nature that can be harnessed? Controlled? Imagine if it were something we could induce rather than endure."

"I fail to see the advantage."

"Really? As a soldier I had thought you would. Think of all the places where man is at a disadvantage, the hottest deserts, the deepest oceans. Imagine if he could adapt to that environment, embrace it rather than be threatened by it. There is no country we could not fight in, no battlefield on which we would not dominate."

The thought was so repugnant to me that I confess I could not reply for a few moments. Was there no limit to the arrogance of man?

"It is not our place to play God, Mycroft," I said at last.

"Ah," he replied with a smile. "What a pleasure it must be to have the luxury of morals. They are things I have had to abandon long ago. In my position, Doctor, you must appreciate that *nothing* is beyond contemplation. It's all very well my objecting to a principle but what use will that be when the Germans mobilise troops that have a biological advantage over our own? Much comfort my principles will be when our men are dying."

"But surely someone has to draw a line. Must we all submit to our basest thoughts? Entertain the very worst behaviour just in case our neighbour does the same?"

"Welcome to my world, Doctor."

"If we could agree to accept the pragmatic nature of your work and move on to the facts?" Holmes suggested, impatient as always to get to the actual data.

"Indeed," Mycroft agreed, clearly happy to do just that. "Though I will just say that perhaps the doctor would not be quite so affronted by the idea were its medical applications appreciated. Imagine a body evolved beyond the reach of disease – the principle is just the same. In fact I believe that was the initial route taken by the specialist I had contracted to explore the possibility."

Catching a look from my friend begging me to interject no further, I sank back into my seat and let Mycroft speak.

"I'm sure you do not need me to tell you of Dr Charles Moreau," he continued, and the images brought out by mention of that man's name did little to improve my mood.

Charles Moreau had been a prominent and extraordinary physiologist, a man with a reputation for fresh and exciting scientific thoughts as well as a quick temper when it came to expressing them. His fall from grace was sudden and – in my opinion at least – fully justified. It was also wholly engineered.

A journalist, working under false credentials, had secured a position as Moreau's laboratory assistant. Working alongside the doctor, the journalist was witness to countless vivisection experiments against animals that can have had little grounding in scientific reasoning. Certainly, the pamphlet Moreau prepared discussing his findings – a pamphlet that was to be universally debunked by his peers – couldn't explain the acts reported. Aware that he must justify his position of allowing the cruelty to continue, the journalist claimed that he could not intervene without betraying himself and he wished to gather enough evidence against Moreau to ensure the man's public censure, perhaps even enough to bring criminal proceedings. Whether this is true or simply an attempt on the young man's part to gloss over the fact that he put his desire to get good copy in the way of his moral imperative is neither here nor there.

On the morning of Moreau's planned publication, the assistant allowed one of the animals to escape. It was a small Labrador, partially flayed, covered in surgical wounds and bristling with needles. The animal's howls brought considerable attention. A shocked crowd gathering as they attempted to corner and placate the beast. It was in such a state of terror that a passing cab driver could see no other course than to put the animal out of its misery. It set a spark to months of suspicion and rumour amongst residents of the capital, and eventually a mob descended on his Greenwich home. The atrocities brought out into the daylight that morning damned Moreau's reputation forever.

The journalist published and his editor took the opportunity to tap into public feeling and whip up a wave of anger against the doctor. It seemed to all concerned that the man had finally lost whatever skills he may have once possessed. London became too small to hold him. He left, setting sail for new shores, a mob of protesters jeering him off.

"Don't tell me that Moreau was working for you?" I asked.

"Not to begin with," Mycroft admitted. "But the journalist that exposed him was."

"To begin with?" Holmes asked.

Mycroft smiled. "We must remember that for all his clear faults, Moreau was a genius and, as reprehensible as his methods may have been, there was no doubt that he was on to something potentially fascinating."

"From what I recall," I said, "his published theories were nothing but unscientific tosh. He was a spent force."

"My dear Doctor," Mycroft replied, "you really mustn't believe all you read."

CHAPTER THREE

"I was there," continued Mycroft, "on the night Moreau left our country. I had thoroughly debriefed my agent as to the work Moreau had been conducting. While most of it was, as you say, so removed from practical science as to be evidence of a damaged personality, some was rather more interesting. The work he conducted after, on a small retainer from me, was vitally so.

"The offer I presented was simple. His chances of legitimate practice had been wholly ruined. If he wished to continue in science he would have no choice but to accept the small budget I offered and the direction I wished that research to follow. I wasn't blind to his wilfulness and, once out of the country, there would be a limit to the level of control I could apply. Nonetheless, I supplied him with company – an assistant cum caretaker, a man I had worked with on a handful of occasions previously and whom I thought entirely trustworthy. Perhaps he was, though I now also know he was a drunk and, as can be the way with sufferers of that particular condition, far too easily led if offered a warm bed and a full bottle.

"They worked on a small island in the South Pacific, away from the attentions of civilisation, with nothing but a twice-yearly trip to replenish supplies. They were perfectly isolated. Nothing but the work I offered and the dangled promise of future vindication should that work bear fruit."

"And what was that work?" Holmes asked.

"He was attempting to define the biological trigger for evolutionary change chemically, hoping to isolate and replicate it. The hope was that he might develop some serum or another that could improve our resilience; increase our immunity against disease; make us more impervious to extremes of temperature; or able to function for longer periods without food or water. The sort of small improvements that, frankly, might give an army all the advantage it needed in order to be victorious."

"Why," I exclaimed, "this is incredible! Did you really think such things were possible?"

"My dear Watson," Mycroft replied with some irritation, "I considered such things entirely possible given the work Moreau had already completed. I am not one to waste Her Majesty's money. Sadly, it was not to be. Moreau had other plans.

"One day I simply stopped receiving messages from Montgomery, my agent. I confess my first instinct was to assume a natural disaster had befallen them, a storm perhaps or even an attack by natives. Who was to say what dangers might lurk in so remote a part of the globe? It certainly seemed unlikely that they could survive without my financial assistance."

"Surely you had some method of checking?" Holmes asked.

"I had one of our ships make a casual investigation when sailing past the island. I could hardly allow the crew to know the reason behind my investigation of course. I allowed an order to pass through navy command asking for the area to be assessed for military use. Included within that order was the need to check for signs of habitation. If Moreau, Montgomery and his native retinue were still alive then I felt sure they would betray the fact somehow, a trace of fire-smoke, fishing paraphernalia on the beach, something must certainly alert the crew. Of course, if they had been found, then my security would likely have been compromised, but I deemed it worth the risk. Uppermost in my mind at all times was the possibility that Moreau had sold his work to another power. Needless to say that is always a risk and one that I would have dealt with to the best of my ability had it arisen. Perhaps it has…"

"You have heard from Moreau?" Holmes asked.

"Nothing so simple," his brother replied. "But this matter is complicated. Let me continue it in a strict manner.

"In total, Moreau was unheard of for eight years. Then, twelve years ago, the *Lady Vain* sank in the South Pacific, perhaps you remember?"

Indeed I did. The ship had collided with a derelict vessel only a few days out from Callao and, aside from a crammed longboat – later rescued by a navy vessel – all other passengers were lost. I recounted as much to Mycroft.

"All other passengers bar one," he replied. "Edward Prendick, a wealthy young man who had taken to the study of natural history, as all wealthy men must take to the study of something unless they wish to lose their minds before they are thirty. He was found eleven months after the loss of the *Lady Vain*, adrift in that patch of ocean."

"He survived out there for eleven months?"

"Indeed not, that would have been exactly the sort of feat of endurance I was paying Moreau to accomplish. Prendick claimed to have spent the time between the sinking of the *Lady Vain* and his later rescue on an island in the company of the disgraced Moreau, the drunk Montgomery and a collection of monstrous creatures, the like of which had him branded delusional before he had even reached port."

"What sort of creatures?" I asked.

"Hybrids – absurd combinations of man and beast – the results, he claimed, of Moreau's experiments in vivisection. He insisted that the island had become colonised by them, an entire culture of educated animals, walking upright like men. The creatures had risen up against their creator, with Prendick being the lone survivor."

I laughed. "And Holmes accuses me of being far-fetched in my ideas," I replied. "Even I wouldn't dream of a story so wild."

Mycroft met my incredulity with stony silence. Eventually he spoke. "Far-fetched or not, Prendick was telling the truth."

I was quite unable to respond seriously to that. Even Holmes looked startled, staring at his brother through a slowly exhaled mouthful of smoke, perhaps to judge his sincerity. For myself I was in no doubt of that. Mycroft was not a man inclined to lie – though, on reflection, as a secret-service man he must have been perfectly adept at it. When talking to Holmes he was only too aware of the importance of precise facts. If he said a thing was the case, then it was. But how were animal-human hybrids even remotely possible? I couldn't help but think he must have been mistaken. No doubt Moreau – a man clearly in love with both the scalpel and wild flights of imagination – had constructed a selection of *faux* creatures, like the monstrosities one hears of in American travelling shows. What had made such an impression on Prendick can have been no more than the absurd "fish-boys" and "bird-ladies" of the freak show. No doubt, to an untrained eye, such things might pass muster. I suggested as much to Mycroft but the large man simply shook his head.

"I can understand your scepticism," he said. "As you are a man of medical science I would be disappointed should you offer anything else. However, I can prove the veracity of everything, and perhaps it would save time if you were simply to accept my words at face value!"

Which put me in my place.

"It is clear that Moreau felt that the answer to my scientific problem lay in continuing his exploration of vivisection. Perhaps he felt that animal attributes couldn't be conferred upon humans on a chemical level, they must be grafted on with needle and twine. Either that or he simply couldn't leave the scalpel alone. I think that's equally possible."

"Some people just can't resist spilling blood," I agreed. "There is a power in interfering with nature that some broken individuals should not be entitled to wield."

"Whatever the truth of the matter, science can never move backwards. Once knowledge is acquired it can only grow, not vanish again into ignorance."

"But, surely, if Moreau died…?"

"I am by no means sure he did. Prendick's account is unequivocal on the matter. He says the beasts tore their creator apart. He and Montgomery disposed of the body themselves. Montgomery was attacked later and his body – presumed dead at least – was thrown into the sea."

"'*Presumed* dead'?" Holmes asked.

"I'm being as accurate as possible. We must bear in mind that we only have one man's word to go on for any of it."

"One man who I presume has stood up to rigorous debriefing," I commented.

"Not that rigorous," Holmes added. I looked at him and he qualified his statement with a brief smile. "He hasn't talked to me."

"Nor is he likely to," Mycroft said. "Edward Prendick is dead. Bear in mind this all happened eleven years ago. Finding the hustle and bustle of town too much for nerves frayed by his experiences, he repaired to the countryside. He devoted himself to chemistry and reading, living the life of a hermit. Which is why it was a couple of days before his body was found." Mycroft drained what was left of his coffee and perched the cup and saucer on the arm of his chair. "Evidence points towards his having committed suicide. Certainly that was the decision made by the courts."

"You doubt it?" Holmes asked.

"Only because I cannot imagine a skilled chemist committing suicide by drinking acid. There are less painful ways to achieve oblivion."

"It would seem unnecessarily agonising," I agreed. "Surely a narcotic would be likelier. Were the remains so corrupt that positive identification was impossible?"

"He was not in a fine state, naturally, but the police were satisfied as to his identity. He was recognised by the postmaster, the man who it would seem knew him best as he regularly had to collect parcels of scientific equipment."

"So," Holmes said, "we have three people who might possess the knowledge to replicate these experiments in vivisection. All of them are, on the surface at least, dead. The fact that you refuse to accept that means these experiments are continuing – correct?"

"I have my suspicions," his brother agreed. "You will have been following, no doubt, the news coverage of the Rotherhithe deaths?"

"Several bodies found in or near the river," Holmes said. "Police reports stated that they were the result of gang violence."

"Well they would, wouldn't they?" Mycroft replied. "Nothing keeps the inquisitive nature of a populace down more than mention of gang violence."

"It certainly bored Holmes at the time," I admitted. "I tried to interest him in it but he refused to listen."

"I don't believe you ever mentioned it."

This angered me. I was forever reading Holmes news reports in the hope of sparking his curiosity.

"I read out half the paper!" I insisted.

He shrugged. "If my memory serves, and it usually does, there was not one single crime I could have investigated."

I wasn't having that, and wracked my brain for that day's top recommendations: "There were several burglaries; the assassination of Charles DuFries; that greyhound trainer, Barry Forshaw, vanished mid-race; the Highgate poisonings, the robbery on the 12.05 to Leamington and the kidnap of a Parisian furrier," I said.

He dismissed the lot with the flick of his hand.

"Trifles!" he shouted. "Missing persons and pilferers!"

I looked to Mycroft. "For someone who complains of boredom so easily you have no idea how difficult it is to get him to engage in an actual case. On that particular day he threw the paper in the fire and got on with cataloguing his collection of dog hair."

"Dog hair?" Mycroft raised an eyebrow.

"How else can one expect to recognise a breed by only a few strands?" Holmes replied.

Mycroft allowed that thought to hover in the air for a moment before continuing with his story. "If we can return to Rotherhithe? The bodies were in fact the result of animal attacks."

"Ah," I replied. "I think I can see where this might fit in."

"Indeed, the pathology reports make it clear that the wounds are not the result of any one animal they can pin their reputations on."

"And we discount the logical answer," Holmes said. "That they were killed by multiple creatures. Why?"

"Because one would tend to think that if there really were a shark in the Thames we would have heard reports of one by now."

"One of the creatures was a shark?"

"The latest cadaver had had its left leg bitten off by a blacktip shark, a species most commonly found off the coast of Australia."

"Absurd!" I exclaimed.

"Fascinating," Holmes announced, turning to look at me. "A few weeks ago you were willing to believe in the existence of demons and the efficacy of magic. Now, when presented with science – albeit of a peculiar and hitherto unheard of variety – you blanch at the thought. It says a great deal about you."

"In the matter of The Breath of God I simply chose to accept the evidence of my own senses," I countered.

"A cardinal error," Holmes replied. "Unless aggressively trained, senses can be easily cheated."

"So you believe all this madness about monsters abroad in the streets of Rotherhithe?"

"I neither believe nor disbelieve it." He nodded towards Mycroft. "Much like my brother I am sure. I would not believe a thing until I absolutely knew it to be the case. However, we must accept that the widest reaches of scientific possibility may well turn out to be proven correct. Science is a fluid thing, Doctor. Like mercury spilled on the laboratory table, it chases away with itself. Often it is quite beyond us to restrain or capture it."

"I am aware of the nature of science, Holmes," I replied with irritation. "I have spent a number of years studying it after all."

"Indeed," Holmes said, offering a placating smile. "And you have considerable talent in your field."

"In my field." I smiled, unable to resist dwelling on his caveat. "Indeed."

"I make no firm conclusions," Mycroft said. "I simply present everything I know to be relevant, and trust in your skills –" he looked at me "– both of your skills – to help get to the bottom of things. I want you to investigate the deaths, eradicate – or confirm – alternative explanations, and act on them."

"Act on them?" asked Holmes.

"If Dr Moreau is alive and well and working in the capital, I want him found."

I laughed. "From everything you've said, one would think you were more in need of game hunters than a detective."

"I have them too," Mycroft replied. "This is too important a matter to entrust to only two men."

Holmes scoffed at that and kicked at the leg of his chair with his heel. He was not a man who relished the idea of working as part of a team.

"I know how much you enjoy working with others, Sherlock," Mycroft said. "But you will simply have to accept that this is a wide-reaching matter and I have set all of my best men on it."

"'All'?" Holmes positively shouted this. "How many is 'all'?"

"You need not be in each others' pockets throughout the

investigation but as well as an expert in hunting and tracking I have instigated a little… Well, let us call it a science club. I have charged the best brains in the country to look to the matter and offer their input. Who knows whether we will need biological assistance, or medical, or simply someone to approach the scientific aspects of the case in a more lateral manner? You'll meet them later this evening. I've told them to expect you."

"At the clubhouse?" I asked with a smile.

Mycroft chuckled. "Indeed, the most perfect place you could imagine for such a club. They are in residence at The British Museum."

CHAPTER FOUR

I had visited The British Museum before of course. Most recently, I had taken Mary there for a dull afternoon when rain had forced us indoors and away from the lake in Regent's Park. I say "dull" not because I had no interest in its collections, but everything has its time and place and reading about Egyptian excavations will never be a replacement for lolling on the water with the woman you love.

Holmes and I descended from our cab at five minutes to the appointed hour and made our way along Great Russell Street.

"I sometimes wonder," Holmes said as we turned the corner into Montague Street, "whether this is not the repository of some of the greatest crimes of our time. Thefts far beyond the paltry affairs I concern myself with – national treasures, chunks of history, all whipped away to be stowed, under lock and key, in the name of education and empire."

"But surely," I replied, "archaeology is hardly theft. We have discovered some of the finest historical artefacts in the world, preserved them, learned from them."

"They are rare lions," he said, gazing up at the building, "torn from their natural jungle to rot away in the smoke-filled streets of an alien land."

He was bordering on the poetic, something that always put me on edge with Holmes! It could be a sign of mania – either excessive exuberance or the most terrible depression. Not that I was completely immune to the atmosphere of the place. After hours, the building had a decidedly eerie quality. Gone was the hubbub of school parties and black-frocked nannies poking their unwilling charges through the doors. The light was dim and the shadows in the colonnaded entrance seemed unnaturally dense. Perhaps my nerves were still raw from our most recent case, but I will admit to being chilled by more than just the January air as we made our way towards the main entrance.

Holmes jogged up the steps to the main doors and rapped on the wood with the head of his cane. He turned and smiled, looking not unlike one of the rare lions he had mentioned earlier.

After a few moments there was the sound of a bolt being drawn and a lock being turned. The door opened a crack and the face of an elderly caretaker appeared in the gap.

"Mr Holmes?" the old man asked.

"Indeed," Holmes replied, tipping his hat, "and my colleague Dr John Watson."

"Of course, Sir," the caretaker replied. "I was told to expect both of you." He opened the door fully and there was a waft of hair-oil and dust. "You will forgive me, Sirs, if I check your credentials. Matters here are of such a delicate nature that it's more than my job's worth to let just anyone in."

"You may have my card, certainly," I replied, trying to keep the irritation from my voice. I could quite understand the gentleman's need for security but I have never responded well to such behaviour.

"With all due respect, Sir," he smiled, "a man's card is easily attained. I had something more reliable in mind." He turned to Holmes. "Tell me, Sir: 'Whoever makes it, tells it not. Whoever takes it, knows it not. Whoever knows it, wants it not.' What am I describing?"

I sighed and tapped impatiently at the steps with my cane. "We have an appointment," I said. "We were not warned it was with the damned Sphinx."

Holmes held up his hand. "I don't mind." Nor would he – any chance to show off his reasoning. He repeated the man's riddle, shrugged as if it were child's play itself. "I presume you are describing counterfeit currency?"

The old man smiled and stepped back. "Indeed, Sir, please be so good as to enter."

Holmes did so but, as I prepared to follow, the old man interceded again. "Forgive me, Sir," he said, "but you will likewise have to answer a question."

"Dear Lord!" I rolled my eyes. "I can't stand word games and riddles, this is utterly preposterous."

"I wouldn't dream of offering you a riddle, Sir," he replied, "my questions are naturally intended to confirm a person's identity and are catered very specifically to their skills." He looked skyward, scratching his light beard as he thought for a moment. "Ignoring the phalanges and the metacarpus –" he leaned forward and smiled "– such are common terms and far too easy even for the layman – name four bones within the human hand."

"Scaphoid, carpus, trapezium and ulna."

I made to push past him but he held up his hand. "I think you'll agree, Sir, that the ulna is located in the arm rather than hand."

I was growing to hate this man. Though he was quite right. I never had liked exams, they flustered me. "Triquetral!" I shouted.

"Just so, Sir," he concurred, allowing me past. "You could also have had capitate or lunate of course."

If this irritating man didn't get on with it, I would be sorely tempted to show him the bones in my own hand, with some force. Perhaps this showed for, once inside the building, the elderly fellow took pains not to delay us further.

"The other gentlemen," he explained, "are waiting for you in the Reading Room. I try not to leave them alone together for too long – they are wont to begin fighting."

"Fighting?" What manner of meeting was this?

"I am of the opinion, Sir, that there is nothing more violent than the scientific community. They are always so set in their ideas, ideas their colleagues rarely share." Heading towards the main door of the Reading Room he gave a chuckle, releasing it suddenly and percussively, as if it were the product of pent-up wind. "And there are few in the community whose ideas are more divergent than this lot," he said, opening the door just as a large volume of Homer's verse came sailing through it.

"How dare you, Sir!" came a voice from inside, deep and loud, the sort of voice a boulder might possess if given speech. "Nobody dismisses the work of George Edward Challenger and leaves the room with his teeth still in his mouth!" The man was a giant. Never had I seen a man with a head so damnably large! If he kept it full he must be a clever man indeed. The rest of his body was built to carry such an intimidating skull, huge and muscular, with a paunch that showed his appetite was as big as the rest of him.

"Don't be a barbarian!" cried a high-pitched voice from the shadows beneath a desk. The giant's opponent was his opposite in almost every way. Though not particularly short he was wiry and spare, with gangly limbs that looked worryingly snappable when seen within a few feet of Challenger's massive hands. The man's small, pink face peered out, myopic eyes squinting through thick spectacles, a moustache twitching in fright like the whiskers of a dormouse. "I was merely theorising!"

"Theorising?" Challenger climbed atop another desk, holding his arms up in the air like a gorilla championing its right to be dominant male. "What a lily-livered little flea you are, Cavor! Stand up for yourself like a man."

"I'd rather not," the man cried, "for if I do you'll most certainly bash my head in!"

"Gentlemen!" cried a third man, coming out from behind the cover of one of the bookshelves. This man was not dissimilar to Cavor, though considerably older and more dishevelled. He wore fingerless gloves and his pince-nez were as crooked as his colourful bow tie. "We really don't have time for these sorts of childish shenanigans. I have left my work at a critical stage in order to attend this meeting and I think the least the rest of you could do would be to keep matters brief and to the point."

"Work?" scoffed a fourth voice. This next man was more urbane in appearance, though his red cheeks and clenched fists suggested he had a temper as quick to flare as Challenger's. Given his advanced years, one couldn't in all conscience encourage anger in him. He was eighty if he was a day, and as frail as one would expect of someone that age. "You're an idiot, Perry, and little more than an engineer. Why we indulge your presence at these meetings I'll never know!"

"Engineer?" Perry raised his wool-wrapped fists and adopted a pugilistic stance. "How dare you! At least my work has a practical application! The Perry Thumping Jenny! The Perry Force Wand! The Perry Hound Vaccination Pipe! What have you got to show for yourself, eh Lindenbrook?"

"I have travelled to the very centre of the Earth!" Lindenbrook countered.

"So you say," Perry replied. "But where's the evidence, eh? You impressed those fools in Hamburg, but you don't impress me!"

"Please, Sirs." The caretaker stepped into the middle of the room and raised his hands in a placatory fashion. "Your first guests have arrived and the Reading Room is hardly the place for fisticuffs. With all respect to your combined intelligence, you stand to damage countless centuries of learning with every blow."

"Aye," said Challenger, looking over to Holmes and I, "well, perhaps we can continue our discussion later, Cavor. It would hardly be seemly to brawl in front of our illustrious guests."

The small man stayed under the table. He was muttering to himself and running his finger through the dust on the floor. Challenger shook his head in despair and made his way over to us. "Ignore Mr Cavor. He is often stricken by a sudden need to indulge in formulae. He'll always have his head in the clouds."

"Surely that would make it lighter than air?" the aforementioned Cavor asked, seemingly of nobody in particular.

"My name is George Edward Challenger," Challenger announced, grasping each of us firmly by the hand. "Leading anthropologist and one of the finest scientific minds of our age."

"We're lucky to make your acquaintance," I replied, with a hint of humour.

"Indeed you are," he replied, with none of that humour returned. "Allow me to introduce my colleagues." He gestured towards Lindenbrook. "This is Professor Lindenbrook, specialises in antiquarian study, cryptology and geology. You may be familiar with his name from a story published thirty odd years ago. He claimed to have visited the centre of the Earth with his nephew."

Holmes raised his eyebrow.

"No? Says he saw prehistoric creatures there," Challenger continued.

"I feel sure I would recall such a tale," Holmes replied, in a manner that was surprisingly polite.

"You would, wouldn't you?" Challenger replied with a smile. "But then, despite an initial flurry of interest in Hamburg – the most naive city in the world it would seem – the scientific journals have not seen fit to trouble the professor for more information."

"Arrogant ape," Lindenbrook spluttered. "I know what I saw! I will not be mocked in this manner!"

Challenger simply smiled and grabbed the man in his thick arms. "Oh hush, Professor! We don't think you're mad really." He winked at us over the old man's shoulder. "It's a shame you don't have the forcefulness of George Edward Challenger. I can assure you, if I'd seen the things you claim to have done then the world would be my oyster!"

"Insufferable man," Lindenbrook replied, trying to release himself from what was not so much an embrace as a wrestling manoeuvre.

"Abner Perry," announced the scruffy man, extending his woollen-clad hands to Holmes and I in turn, "inventor, logician and dreamer." He gave a little laugh and grasped his lapels, which promptly ejected twin plumes of dust.

"Jumped-up blacksmith!" Lindenbrook insisted, finally breaking free of Challenger's grip.

Perry chose not to rise to the bait this time, but simply removed a small metal canister from his pocket. "You are familiar no doubt with the Perry Canine Remonstration Pod?" He raised it to his lips and blew into it. "Somewhere a dog is very sorry for being so boisterous. If only it worked on professors."

He took out a long piece of pipe and extended it, a telescopic mid-section stretching to several feet. "Or the Perry Dust Vaporisation Baton? It requires an acid jar by way of a power source, but fries dust in hard-to-reach places. It smells like the final circle of Hell, but I find it stops the housekeeper from offering her notice quite so often."

A small glass bottle followed. He uncorked it, took a sip and replaced it in his jacket pocket.

"And that?" I asked. "The Perry Effervescent Tonic?"

"In a way," he replied. "My doctor insists I take it to keep me regular. I suffer from a nervous bowel."

"And finally," Challenger interrupted, "we have Mr Cavor, the thin wastrel you saw me remonstrating with when you came in. He's a physicist and shortly to be owner of a broken neck unless he watches his tongue around me."

"The issue of gravity should be a small one," muttered Cavor, still under the desk, "if only the correct ratio could be maintained."

"Come out, Cavor!" bellowed Challenger, kicking at the leg of the table and knocking the physicist out of his daydream. "We have company."

"Oh yes!" said Cavor. "Company – yes." He stepped out and walked up to us. I was somewhat startled to realise he was considerably younger than I had assumed. Perhaps no more than thirty. His thick moustache, light hair and manner had led me to assume him much older. "Company," he said again, looking at us both. "I'm sorry, do I know you?"

"Dr John Watson," I said, extending my hand, "and this is my colleague Sherlock Holmes."

He shook my hand. "I don't think I do," he said. "I'd remember a name like Sherlock, certainly. Is it about the rent?"

I assured him not.

"Oh good," he said. "I've spent this month's allowance on mercury you see, and was worried we were about to have something of an argument. I don't really like arguments." He smiled and wandered off, making a high-pitched whine that I would later discover seemed to form an undercurrent to most of his idle thoughts.

"Yes," said Challenger, only too aware of the impression they had all made. "Well, genius often ousts the social niceties. It is so hard to fit everything into a brain after all."

On this point he found himself in unspoken agreement with Holmes, who nodded and smiled. "One must concentrate on the tools one needs," he said. "What use are social niceties when it comes to creating a new element, exploring a hitherto undiscovered jungle, inventing a new device?"

"Or identifying a pernicious criminal?" Challenger added with a wide grin. I found myself nervous to see so many of his teeth – I couldn't help but imagine them clamping down on my leg like those of a voracious tiger.

"Indeed!" Holmes agreed.

There was the distant sound of a knock on the door and the elderly caretaker sighed and left the room. "Oh for the peaceful nights when it's just me and the Egyptian dead," he muttered.

"Ah!" said Challenger. "That will be our trigger finger."

"I'm sorry?" I asked, confused as to his meaning.

"We are the brains," he explained, "the scientific backbone of the operation. But the brain needs a strong arm, a fist, to enact its commands."

He led us to the central table where several large maps of the city had been unfurled. "Mr Holmes –" he glanced at my friend "– that is, the other Mr Holmes, has charged us with the scientific part of the investigation. Despite our apparent irritations…"

"Nothing 'apparent' about it," Lindenbrook muttered. "I think you're horrible!"

"Despite that," Challenger continued, "we have had some success in the past working together on Departmental problems. This is somewhat outside our field it must be said, but Lindenbrook and I do at least have a sound knowledge of zoology and practical experience of nature at its most bizarre and dangerous. Combining that with Perry and Cavor's more abstract approach we hope to be able to theorise productively, narrowing down the zoological evidence. We are trying to identify the species involved and how such creatures might best be preserved in the metropolis."

"That would certainly seem to be the obvious starting point for investigation," Holmes agreed. "One doesn't hide a menagerie in a city without leaving evidence."

"That's our hope," Challenger agreed. "But then we're approaching this from the point of view of the creature, or creatures. I assume you are planning on pursuing the man?"

"That would seem to be the obvious route for my skills to take, yes," agreed Holmes.

The caretaker returned. "Gentlemen," he announced, "Mr Roger Carruthers."

The new arrival removed his hat and extended his hand to each of us in turn. "Pleased to meet you, I'm sure," he said. "You may be familiar with my recently published journal of life in the Andes?"

"Can't say I am," Challenger replied. "But you come highly recommended so I shouldn't let it worry you."

"Oh," Carruthers replied, clearly disheartened. "It was rather well received. Perhaps my account of a journey along the Tigris, *A Meander in Mesopotamia*?"

"We don't have time for popular reading," Lindenbrook snapped. "We're proper scientists, not the sort of bored housewives who get a thrill from the mention of intimate piercings in savages."

"Well," Carruthers replied, "I can assure you it was highly regarded in all walks of life. In fact the Royal Society said…"

"Oh, the Royal Society will say anything," laughed Challenger. "But please don't concern yourself. You are in the company of busy men, men whose researches often keep them away from the latest reading."

"The problem will be one of stability!" Cavor announced, before emitting a strange whining noise. Carruthers stared at him, clearly convinced he had found himself trapped within a room full of lunatics, or worse – lunatics who had never read his work. I decided to take pity on him.

"John Watson," I said, shaking his hand, "a fellow writer and doctor of medicine."

"Of course!" he exclaimed. "Naturally I've read a great deal of your work!"

"Then you will be familiar with my colleague, Mr Sherlock

Holmes," I replied, gesturing to Holmes before Carruthers could inquire as to whether I was as familiar with his writing as he seemed to be with mine.

"Naturally!" Carruthers replied, shaking Holmes' hand with such vigour I was concerned he may break it. Either that or my friend, not always at his best when faced with cheerful enthusiasm, might beat him off with his cane. Before this might happen, I introduced Carruthers to the rest of the gathered gentlemen, keeping him moving quickly enough that we avoided creating further arguments, even when – taking note of Challenger's girth – Carruthers enquired as to whether he would be interested in membership of the West Highbury Gourmands, an eating club of which he was a founder member.

"Well," he announced, having met everyone, "I believe you want me to shoot something?"

Expressed in such innocent simplicity, the statement had the effect of quieting the whole room, something I might have thought impossible. Noting this, Carruthers was quick to address any inadvertent embarrassment he may have caused.

"Forgive me," he said, "I appreciate I may be oversimplifying matters. But I understood that time was of the essence, and thought it best we get to the point."

"How refreshing that someone has that attitude," said Holmes. "I began to think I might spend all night here."

Ignoring a positively poisonous look from Challenger, Holmes crossed the room towards the door. "Watson and I will leave you to point Mr Carruthers in the correct direction. Should he shoot anything of scientific worth don't hesitate to inform us."

CHAPTER FIVE

"That was rather rude," I said once we were back outside.

"Probably," he agreed, "but I couldn't bear one more minute in their stifling company."

"I did wonder how long you would manage to sit still in there before erupting."

We crossed into Belgravia, Holmes' heart set on an Indian restaurant that lay close by. He ignored all attempts at conversation until we had passed through its nigh-hidden doorway and were sat at one of its opulent, red tables. The smells from the kitchen were heady and sharp, my stomach fairly trembled at the hot, spicy onslaught that would soon be heading its way.

"It has been far too long since we visited here," Holmes announced as the waiter drew close. "Have the kitchens prepare enough for three hungry men," he said. "We'll entrust ourselves to his choice of menu."

The waiter bowed in acknowledgement of the order and walked

away into the gloom, sidestepping his way past the usual mix of retired colonels, medical students and young gentlemen on the wrong side of sobriety.

"Three?" I asked.

"Shinwell Johnson will be meeting us here," Holmes explained. "Given where the bodies were found, it seemed sensible to avail ourselves of his local knowledge."

I'm sure I have mentioned Johnson before. He gave frequent assistance to Holmes after the turn of the century. Originally a criminal of mean repute – with two sentences at Parkhurst to his name – he had repented of his ways and now acted as Holmes' agent within the criminal underworld. He wasn't a "nark", as the vernacular has it, and he never dealt with the police. But he often kept Holmes abreast of movements within the various criminal fraternities, allowing him to know the underbelly of the city like no other. He was an extremely likeable chap once you got beneath the battered brim of his bowler and looked past the broken nose and scarred cheeks.

"Evenin', Gents!" he announced, arriving a few moments later. "One more for dinner?"

"I've ordered for you," said Holmes gesturing to the seat furthest from the door. Johnson was always careful when meeting us in public and liked to make sure he could hide himself away in the shadows.

"Oh, I dare say there's nothing that comes out of that kitchen that could do me a mischief," Johnson replied. "If you'd ever seen my mother's cooking you'd know I'm immune to poison."

Poisonous it was not, though all three of us found ourselves loosening our collars and taking a little more of the claret than we might otherwise have done – anything to try to cool our burning tongues.

"God knows how we ever beat them," said Johnson once he was finished eating. "I feel beaten up just by eating the food."

"Invigorating, isn't it?" said Holmes, taking one last mouthful of something hot and creamy that involved lamb.

"I'll not feel the cold for a week," Johnson agreed. "So –" he reached for his clay pipe "– I'm guessing you want to talk to me about the bodies found in Rotherhithe."

"You guess correctly."

"I thought it would only be a matter of time. In fact, I had half a mind to head over to you myself. I know the papers have been full of rubbish about it being gang violence but, I thought, my Mr Holmes ain't stupid enough to fall for that."

I couldn't help but smile at the uncomfortable look that passed across Holmes' face.

"I confess my attention was elsewhere when the news was first released," he said, "and I didn't give it the attention it clearly deserved."

"You and the rest of London," said Johnson. He smiled, and his good humour was so soft and genuine it transformed his face. "You've got a better excuse than most though," he continued. "One man can only keep his eye on so much after all." He took another mouthful of his drink and lit his pipe. "Probably best if I give you the lot then," he said, "belt and braces, just the way you like it."

CHAPTER SIX

"The first body," Johnson continued, "weren't nothing really. Or so it seemed at the time. You know what it's like – sometimes the patterns are only clear once you can step back and take them all in. Up close they're just a bloody mess. The body was certainly that – more meat than skin, waterlogged and ragged, as frilly as a girl's petticoat. It were found at the docks, bobbing in the water like a kiddie's boat.

"It caused a bit of fuss for a few minutes as people gathered round to watch it get fished out. Then the law turned up, dumped it in a sack and people got back to work. Most folk assumed someone had just fallen in and then been given a going over by one of the boat propellers. It happens from time to time. Besides, it don't take long for anything to turn nasty in the Thames. That water's more alive than most of the folk what live along it if you ask me. Full of disease, rats, and fish what would have your hand off soon as look at you. It's a merciless stretch of water. Once you're in it, it don't like to ever let you go.

"Anyway, the law took the body off and nobody thought any more about it until the next came along.

"It looked as bad as the first but you could tell this one were different. Its hands and feet were chained, for one thing. This wasn't just some drunk who'd stumbled off the jetty, this was someone who had been thrown in.

"People started gossiping then right enough. Was he washed up from a prison ship, they said. Like they were still shipping folk off to Australia or something. Prison ship… I asks you. If there's one thing that will always surprise me, Gentlemen, it's how ruddy thick people can be. If he were a prisoner he must have escaped. Though how he'd have got far, what with the chains, is another question.

"I made it my business to ask around about those chains, Gentlemen, and one thing I can say with some certainty is that they were not prison issue. If there's one thing you can be fairly sure of in that part of the city it's that a good few of its residents know only too well what prison chains look like. So… whoever chained him up did so for reasons other than the law.

"That decided, I made it my business to find out a little more about body number two.

"It was discovered by a bunch of kids… Bless you, Doctor, but you pull a face like that as if the kids round those parts ain't never seen a dead body before. I tell you, my main worry was what the little buggers might have done to it before the police put it under lock and key, I wouldn't trust the sods around there not to sell a few chunks as pie meat! Merciless, they are.

"I paid a visit to a copper friend of mine – I know, I know, there aren't many but he's a decent enough bloke and I've always had time for him just as he's always had time for me. He told me as much as he could find out, which weren't much. The body had been dead before it hit the water – the police surgeon could tell that much. He could also tell that the body had been beaten up before being fed to whatever mad zoo of sharp-toothed buggers it had been. There were distinctive bruise marks that suggested he'd been clubbed. He was still alive when the animals had him though as his hands were fair in pieces, him having raised them to try and fend the monsters off.

"The police surgeon had spent a fair amount of time in India and was sure that he recognised some of the wounds as matching those you'd expect if the bloke had come off on the wrong end of a fight with a tiger. Which is strange, I grant you, but you get all sorts of animals in that neck of the woods, what with the ships and the import businesses. He also identified a number of puncture wounds that he insists are the work of a snake. Again, you get all manner of slithery bastards sneaking free around the docks, though the chill usually kills them off pretty damn quick. I remember, when I were a kid, me old pa bringing home a fat python he'd found. Tasted just like chicken.

"Anyway, all this added up to a pretty rum way of getting dead. Their first assumption – and I have to say it was mine too – was that the victim had broken into one of the less reputable animal exporters. You know what they're like down there. If it ain't animals for toffs, or experiments for those gentlemen of science who haven't the paperwork to get things done right, then it's the Chinks and their medicines. Not that I've got anything against that. I don't see how a tiger's diddly in soup can add years to me life but I'll eat anything once – twice if I like it.

"So I reckoned it was worth asking around to see what was what in that line of trade. And I tell you, they're all as crooked as my gran when the gin money was in. Still, accounting for the fact that I wouldn't trust none of 'em to look after a Jack Russell, let alone a lion, there seems to be two that are particularly known for that perfect combination of scale and corruption – they're big business and they're run so far on the wrong side of the law they're coming back to meet it. So, if it comes down to an animal dealer being involved I'll stake my reputation on it being one or the other.

"The first is a sour old Eyetie goes by the name of Mario – don't they all? His main business is private homes – finding that special something for the Lord and Lady what has everything. Though why you'd ever want a rhino in your backyard I don't rightly know, but the story is he's sold two: one to a nob in Bath the other to a mad Scotchman. How the Hell he shipped 'em in then got them to the client without anyone cottoning on, I don't know. But there you are, he's good at his game, and that's a fact. He also supplies nasty stuff to those silly sods who get a kick out of that sort of thing. You know the sort, Mr Holmes. Jumped up little gangsters what haven't the muscle to scare people without getting all theatrical. End up keeping a cellar full of hyenas or a fish tank full of sharks just to scare the locals. In my day we just used to break your ruddy fingers not shove a rare viper down your trousers. I blame the music hall – gives people a taste for showing off. He might be your man – if there's even a connection – but my money's on number two.

"Number two's a Taff, goes by the name of Thomas – don't they all? Does a lot of his business with the scalpel brigade, which is why I think he's your man. Most of his animals are nothing but pelt and a bucket full of lights before he's finished counting his money. Doctors buy 'em. Scientists buy 'em. Anyone who fancies seeing what the poor things look like on the inside buys 'em. Can't pretend to understand why. Doctor cutting up a cadaver's one thing – I can see how he needs to learn his way around. Still, you can plot your way from a badger's arse to his top set but it ain't going to help me when I'm on the operating table, is it?

"So, those are your likely suspects if you want to go down that route. Though I have to say that neither are the sort that would draw attention to themselves by dumping the bodies elsewhere. I mean, if you've got a leopard in the cellar then you've no worries getting rid of a dead body have you? It'll be nothing but chewed bones within minutes. Still, rare animals come into play somehow, so I've given you the gen.

"Body three – now that turned up not two days ago. The main difference there is he weren't floating down the river, he was found in a small pile of himself dumped in the corner of the Bucket of Lies. That's not the pub's real name of course, it's the Bouquet of Lilies but as most of the people what drink there can't read, especially on their way out, the name sort of shifted. Suits it better and all, the only time you'd catch a whiff of lilies there is if one of the regulars had been grave-robbing.

"The body was found by a blind man what picked it up thinking it was his own belongings! You shouldn't laugh but there you go, there's not much to put a smile on your face in that part of the city. So you takes your chuckles, as black as they may be, wherever you find 'em. He only realised his mistake when he felt his back getting wet. There weren't much blood left in the body, not with the chunks it had missing, but what there was soon dripped through the sacking and his shirt. He fair terrified the residents of the Bucket of Lies when he walked back in and asked, 'Which one of you gits spilled beer in my bag, then?' – upturning the sack so all the contents were spilling over the bar. He was furious when somebody finally explained what it was he'd been carrying around, not because he was squeamish – he were an old veteran from what I understand, and it takes a lot to get a soldier's lip to tremble as well you know, Dr Watson. Nah, he was kicking up a fuss because he'd gone from wet belongings to no belongings at all. They never did find his sack, poor sod.

"Now, as you two know, by the time you get to three bodies, people really start to take an interest. Not just the police, I'm talking about the papers. There's nothing sells the gossip sheets better than a bit of spilled blood. Let's be honest – if they could use that instead of ink they would. They're a savage bunch, journalists, and no mistake.

"So before the stains on the bar at the Bucket of Lies have so much as dried, people who have never been within spitting distance of the place are talking about it. The gossip starts, the theories, the lies, the stories getting bigger with each retelling. It's the sort of thing that drives any self-respecting copper off his nut – if there is such a thing as a self-respecting copper, and it takes all sorts so I suppose there must be. How can you conduct a decent investigation once the gossip kicks off, eh? Everyone's got a story to tell and half of them have made it up.

"So, before you know it, the main thing becomes a need to make the story shrivel up and go away. It'll happen in time anyway – the public are never interested in anything for long. But if the whole lot can be written off as quickly as possible nobody need panic, and our city's police force can get back to looking like they know what they're doing. Besides, it's not as if anyone important died now is it? Dropping like flies down there anyway, ain't they – nothing so disposable as the working classes. So everyone starts talking about gangs fighting amongst themselves, and the newspapermen yawn and move on to something more interesting.

"But it ain't the gangs, Mr Holmes, none that I know of anyway, and I keep my ear to the ground as you know, so there's not much that gets past me on that score. We've had two new faces over the last few months, an Irishman who seems to have a political axe to grind more than an urge to make any real money, and an enigmatic sort by the name of Kane who keeps himself to himself. Haven't so much as clapped eyes on him but he's got some clout and has won a few boys over. I can't see either of them having anything to do with this though, can you? This sort of thing's no use unless people know who done it. A gang don't top a bloke in such an over-the-top way unless they're making a point, and if they're making a point they open their gobs about it, stands to reason. Nah, this ain't nothing to do with the gangs and I'd stake my reputation on it. Which in fact, I just have.

"Whatever's going on here – and I have no doubt that if anyone can get to the bottom of it, I'm talking to him, Mr Holmes – then it's a lot darker and nowhere near as simple as bloody 'gang violence.'"

CHAPTER SEVEN

If I hadn't felt full after my meal, I certainly did after Johnson's talk. He had a way of speaking that assaulted both the ears and brain. God knows how Holmes, a man who saw the strict delineation of facts as perfection itself, managed to filter what he needed out of it. Nonetheless he always seemed to manage.

"Plenty to be going on with there, I think," he said. "I may well call on you again. This strikes me as a case where local knowledge – or perhaps just a strong right fist – will be frequently needed."

"I'm here whenever you need me, Mr Holmes," Johnson replied. "You know that."

Holmes paid for our meal and announced that a short walk would do us both good.

"We must decide our next step, Watson," he said. "And the cold air will energise us to do just that."

Shinwell Johnson left us the minute we had stepped out of the restaurant, slipping away almost mid-sentence to return to the world he knew so well but which was alien to us. As we walked the streets of Belgravia, Holmes was mostly silent, digesting the facts of the case as well as our meal. Every now and then he would tap out a rhythm on the pavement slabs with his cane, or stop to stare in the window of a shop, the very figure of a relaxed man about town. I knew he was cogitating furiously beneath the surface, however – a swan with urgent, pedalling feet.

"There is nothing to be gained by observing from afar," he announced after a while, gazing up at the hazy sky above us. "We must make an expedition into enemy territory."

"A trip to Rotherhithe?"

"Certainly." He smiled and looked at me. "Will you come?"

"It makes a change for you to ask." Usually it was all I could do to find out where it was he vanished to in the small hours, leaping – so very unnecessarily – from his bedroom window leaving nothing but the trace of old tobacco and thickly applied spirit gum.

"I know how much you like wandering around the streets with a concealed weapon," he replied, glancing at my jacket pocket, no doubt checking whether I was carrying it now. I wasn't.

"In your company I have frequently had occasion to use it."

"What a good thing it is that the police force owe us a certain latitude."

"How else would their inspectors keep their reputations?" There could be little doubt that Holmes' existence accounted for a fair proportion of the law courts' business.

"It's hardly that," he replied, "what with you blowing the whistle on them every week in your stories. Frankly I'm surprised you'll find a man in uniform to give you the time of day."

"It's you that patronises them, not me."

"A contentious point – your pen…"

"Your words."

"Sometimes." Once again, I was being poked at by an editor.

"Always," I insisted. "Just not necessarily quoted in the right context."

"Misrepresentation."

"Dramatic licence," I sighed. "And my stories have made the entire English-speaking world regard you as a genius. So if you class that as misrepresentation, I'll be happy to make you seem more idiotic next time."

He laughed. "Why not? It might at least give our postal service a rest."

"You couldn't bear it."

"Nonsense! The work is its own reward."

"I believed that of you once," I replied. "Then I noticed how often you liked to announce a man's occupation just by looking at his trouser cuffs."

"Observation."

"Showing off," I smiled.

"There is a difference between explaining method to those intellectually incapable of making their own conclusions, and 'showing off'!" he shouted. And just like that, friendly banter had become earnest – one could never tell with Holmes.

"Indeed there is," I asserted. "One employs humility."

My friend was silenced, if only for a moment. "Very well," he announced finally, his voice as petulant as that of a child, "I shall no longer explain myself and the responsibility falls on you to keep up!"

With that he marched into the road in search of a cab.

CHAPTER EIGHT

It was hardly the first time I had been at the receiving end of one of Holmes' bad moods. His manner was so changeable, swinging from excitement that bordered on mania to the most impenetrable brown studies. It was inevitable therefore that, as his only friend, I should sometimes see the very worst of him. I will say though that I took these moods with considerably more patience than some might have done. In fact, I have often played them down in my case studies as I didn't want to give them undue importance. For those who spent any time with Holmes (and there were few who did, both by their choice and his reluctance to be in company) the speed with which his manner could change was an integral part of his personality.

During the first years of our marriage, Mary had wondered how I had managed to stand it. "He is a genius," she would admit, "but I am at a loss as to how you could have lived with him." It really wasn't all that difficult and she grew to understand. Some people are just built differently from others. Holmes' mind was a thing of wonder, never to find its match again. But for every leap of deductive brilliance, every astounding piece of analysis, there was a price to be paid. Quite simply, genius has its faults. He exercised that brain of his so much, abused it terribly, that it is no wonder that it repaid him with shifting moods. A man cannot kick a soccer ball between the goalposts with such frequency without occasionally tearing a ligament and suffering from a limp.

The important thing to remember about Holmes is this: the man was brilliant and also the very best friend I ever had. That he could manage to be both sets him apart as a giant amongst men.

This is not to say he couldn't often be extremely annoying.

CHAPTER NINE

"Quite why we need to go to all this fuss is beyond me," I admitted as Holmes set to combing the long, grey wig he had prepared for me.

"I have said I'll offer no explanations," he replied, "though the fact that you'd not last five minutes wandering about the backstreets of Rotherhithe as John Watson MD should be obvious. If you want to thoroughly explore an environment you must immerse yourself in it, you must *belong!*"

That and the fact that Holmes always did like dressing up.

By the time he'd finished I was an itching, irritable mess of false hair and make-up. Looking in the mirror that hung above the fireplace, I found myself face to face with a creature so grimy and hirsute I found it hard to accept him as me, no matter how much my logical mind knew better.

Holmes certainly had an eye for disguise. As I believe I may have mentioned before, his skill when he applied it to himself was not so much to hide his features beneath layer and layer of artificial subterfuge, but rather to adapt himself so as to appear to be someone else entirely. He achieved this trick by posture, intonation and natural expression, just as much as he did make-up. It appeared he had little faith that I might share his ability, as there was so little of John Watson to be seen! I must confess he was probably right to err on the side of caution. I had enjoyed theatricals at school – my Laertes brought a tear to the eye of the old nurse as she stood on hand to offer assistance should the fencing get out of hand – but I can't say it was a skill that came readily. Perhaps it was my time in the army, for certainly the comradeship of soldiers teaches a man to be nothing more or less than himself, but the idea of pretending to be the natural occupier of this beard and hair made me distinctly nervous. I decided to experiment with a limp.

"My dear Watson," came Holmes' voice from the other room, "affecting problems with one's gait is the province of music-hall comics and lousy Richard the Thirds. Kindly walk normally or you'll stand out a mile."

I gritted my blackened teeth in irritation and prepared to ask how he had known I was doing any such thing. Then I held my tongue, damned if I was going to give him the satisfaction.

I looked at myself in the mirror again and experimented with my stance. Clearly I was affecting a personality much older than myself so I should stoop a little and maybe even allow my head to hang a little crookedly. A sharp pain in my neck soon knocked that idea out of me.

"Do nothing to draw attention," Holmes continued, still absent from the room. "People will have no interest in you unless you give them cause to do so. Most people are extremely unobservant, as you know, so rely on that fact. Simply believe that wherever you are, you belong; you are in your element; you are natural and at home. Do that –" he appeared in the doorway, bald, tattooed and dressed in the most terribly stained overcoat "– and you'll never be seen."

"Aye, aye, Cap'n," I replied, in the closest I could manage to a thick Irish brogue, much to his apparent disgust.

CHAPTER TEN

We avoided the unnecessarily ostentatious route of Holmes' bedroom window and instead left Baker Street by the front door. I could tell he was far from content about it, but I made it clear that I had no intention of breaking my legs before we'd even begun. From there it was a long walk to the river. Holmes insisted that one didn't go to all the effort of disguising oneself only to then alight from a taxi-cab at one's destination. I could see his logic but felt we could have at least travelled in comfort halfway there. But then, Holmes was not a man to do things by halves.

He also liked to walk through the city, to remind himself of the beating heart of it; of the twists of its streets and back alleys; the little dramas that played out on each corner. Holmes was not always the most empathetic of men, but it was a failing he was aware of and it was during moments like this that he did his best to compensate. He noted everything about people, not just the usual analysis – reading their personality and environment from traces on their person – but also how they interacted with each other. That was where the real mysteries lay, something he knew only too well. "If only the rest of the world was as logical as me," he once said, "I could solve any crime in a matter of moments. It would be a matter of arithmetic, the inarguable sum of its composite parts. But, no – nothing muddies the waters as much as the human mind." Everybody was different and that, for a detective, is where the hard work comes in.

We couldn't have asked for more variety during that walk. We began in the rarefied air of Mayfair, where the gentlemen experienced fresh air only in brief snatches, moving between the velvet-lined wombs of their carriages and the smoky interiors of their clubs. When Holmes had talked of looking as if we belonged he had not expected us to succeed in that aim here; in fact, we were looked upon with nothing less than open hostility by a number of the doormen and the few passers-by who deigned to waste shoe-leather.

"Move along there," cried one old soldier, stitched up in his serge and braid, swapping the uniform of a foreign field for that of the Mummerset Club, where he could live out his years still tugging a forelock to the ranks above him. "We don't like your sort around here."

The fact that, as an ex-serviceman of sufficient rank, I was perfectly entitled to step through the club's doors was something I chose not to mention. He would never believe me. In fact I had more right to step into its bar than he; with my service record I would have a brandy in my hand within moments whereas he would be out on his ear as an upstart pushing beyond his station in life. What ridiculous games we play and how little it all means in the end! Holmes gave him a theatrical salute and moved along the pavement, chuckling in a decidedly drunken manner. *So much for not drawing attention to yourself*, I thought, as we crossed into the theatre district. Here at least we could claim to belong, two strolling players heading towards their chosen stage.

It was the time of evening when many of the performances were ejecting their audiences back out into the world and the streets were busy with happy patrons and those who took advantage of the fact. We were far from being the only people on the street who seemed a long way from home. The crowds were studded with down-at-heel, grimy faces either calling on the generosity of the passers-by or simply helping themselves from unguarded pockets. As we moved past a small group of toughs, loitering by the Adelphi, I became conscious of allowing my hands to loiter near my coat pockets, ready to snatch at any intruding fingers. It took me a moment to realise that, looking as I did, I was hardly likely to present much of a target. As far as these street Arabs were concerned I was one of them, not a potential victim. It was a strange feeling, to be so removed from one's usual sense of self.

From The Strand it was only a short walk to the river and the next available steamboat.

Pressed hard against the rail, I looked out at our smoky city as we made our way along the Thames. It seemed that no matter how long I lived here, I would never stop finding a different angle from which to view it. It was a city of so many faces, and it showed a different one to each and every one of its citizens. To the gentry it was an austere collection of ancient architecture; to the clerk a place of commerce and bustle; to the lower classes it was a dark and unforgiving mother, a place of soot and death that nonetheless gathered its shadowy skirts around the poor and disenfranchised if they begged hard enough.

Now it was a coastal city, an island of noise and light just out of reach across the choppy waters of the river that had always kept it alive.

"She's a dark and ruinous place," I said, unaware I had spoken aloud until Holmes fixed me with a curious stare.

After a moment he nodded. "On my low days, when it seems that nothing will rise from above the commonplace to engage my attention, I remember where it is we live." He watched the towering factories pass us by. "In this city you are never far away from the extraordinary." He thought for a moment. "Or the terrifying."

CHAPTER ELEVEN

We travelled in silence for the rest of our journey. I continued to watch the passing city while Holmes turned his attention towards our fellow passengers. The boat was far from full at that time of the night, but the people it did carry were, for the most part, in boisterous mood.

By the time we arrived at the docks in Rotherhithe, the main bulk of our fellow passengers had taken to singing a bawdy tune regarding the medical health of an excitable young barmaid called Sadie. I can't say I was familiar with the tune before our journey but it was damnably hard to shake from my head after it. From time to time I even found myself whistling a few bars of it as we pushed our way through the busy quayside. I'm sure it helped me fit in amongst the sailors and warehouse men as they shouted to one another, offloading produce or loading supplies, a seemingly endless to and fro of crates and people. The air was thick with the smell of tar and the creak of old ropes. Everybody seemed to be shouting, though it was so commonplace I ceased to be able to discern a single word – the whole became a background roar of voices. It brought to mind the animal noise of a jungle, all the species calling out to one another.

"Where to first?" I asked Holmes, sticking close by his side.

"I think a drink at the Bucket of Lies, don't you?" he replied, moving easily through the crowd. I watched him stroll away from the waterside, the people naturally parting as he came towards them. He was like a large fish, I thought, sweeping the minnows aside in the current he pushed before him. He didn't fade into the background, no matter what his advice, his personality was too strong for that, but he certainly appeared to belong. I thought again of Charles Darwin's theories and wondered if Holmes might be the ultimate example of them; there seemed to be no environment to which he could not adapt, and which he could not dominate. I let that be some small consolation as we drew close to the tavern in question. After all, anywhere that Shinwell Johnson considered rough was likely beyond my scale of comparison.

As we moved away from the water, the streets became quieter. Ports ignore the clock, there is always someone disembarking or arriving, but once we were in the more residential areas, Rotherhithe's citizens were fewer and farther between. By the time we were outside the Bouquet of Lilies, it stood out a mile, the sound of drunken cheering and singing the only sign of life in the surrounding area.

"Looks charming," I said as we drew towards the front door.

"Oh," Holmes said. "I'm sure we'll manage to get through a glass of wine without having our throats cut."

"Yes, because that's always what I look for in a hostelry."

We stepped inside and muscled our way towards the bar, moving between the drunken regulars. I honestly couldn't tell whether some of them were dancing or fighting. The place stank of stale beer and bodily fluids – from the look of the ale the barman handed to me, the two may have been one and the same. I took a mouthful of it nonetheless, conscious of the need to fit in. Given the state of most of the people in here they must have managed to ingest the stuff. Either that, or people stuck to the gin, preferring to lose their eyes rather than their stomachs. The floor had been cleaned once, I was sure, though maybe not during the reign of our current monarch. The clientele was not the sort to fret about such absurd niceties. Perhaps the stickiness of the floorboards even had its benefits, allowing the tired inebriate to maintain their vertical position like a fly stuck to paper.

I did not like the Bouquet of Lilies. Soon, thanks to Holmes, it would become clear that it didn't like me all that much either.

"So," he announced in a loud voice, "what's this I hear about dead bodies then?"

As investigative enquiries went it was not Holmes at his most subtle.

"And who are you to be asking?" said a ruddy old man on Holmes' left. He had a face that was bent terribly out of shape, not helped by a constant nervous twitch that set his cheeks and nose vibrating. He looked as though he was constantly being punched by an invisible assailant.

"Only curious," Holmes replied. "Came in tonight on the *Spirit of Mayfair*, didn't I? Heard some of the lads talking."

"*Spirit of Mayfair*?" asked another old soak, wiping away thick strings of saliva from his chin. He was so much like a bulldog I wondered if Moreau had made him.

"Aye," Holmes replied. "Been away from home for the best part of a year, haven't I?" He drained his tankard, an act of almost Herculean bravery. "And built up one hell of a thirst in that time." He nodded at the barman and handed over the empty vessel.

"Suppose you've the price of another pint?" the first man asked, twitching the mottled lump of scar tissue I took to be a nose, given its location on his face.

Holmes looked at him. "Maybe I have, if you keep a civil tongue and welcome an old sailor back to shore."

"Can't be too careful," the old man said offering his long-empty tankard. "I'm not a man who likes people snooping around."

"Ain't snooping around," said Holmes, "just interested. Who wouldn't be? Bodies turning up with great chunks missing? You see all sorts out at sea but that ain't the sort of thing you expect to come home to is it? Makes me wonder if this is London I've washed up in or New Guinea!" He laughed at that and the old man joined him, more out of eagerness to see his drink filled than sharing in my friend's affected humour. Holmes passed him a full tankard. "So, you going to tell me about it or not? What's going on? Some sort of animal is it? Bloke I met on the quay reckons someone's let a tiger loose or something."

"Ain't no tiger," the old man replied after taking a large mouthful of his drink. "Tiger ain't going to chew you up and then put the bits what's left in a sack is it?"

"Clever tiger," I added with a laugh, wanting to do my bit.

The old man stared at me. "Who's this?" he asked. "He's got a bigger beard than my old wife."

"Mate of mine, ain't he?" Holmes said. "But he don't get out much." Holmes gave me a meaningful stare. He changed the subject before the old man got too distracted. "All right, so it ain't a tiger.

Still, it's got to be some sort of animal that done for 'em, ain't it? Unless it wasn't as bad a mess as I heard…"

"Oh, it were a mess all right," the old man said. "You've never seen the like."

Holmes scoffed. "Don't be so sure, I've seen sights in my time that would make a horse sick. Just 'cos you landlubbers get yourselves in a twist."

"The thing was in pieces," the old man insisted. "It weren't no body, it were a bag of butcher's meat."

"Like I say then, an animal."

"How's an animal put it in a bag you bloody idiot?" shouted the old man in exasperation at Holmes' apparent stupidity. "It wasn't no animal!"

"Maybe an animal did it then a bloke put it in a bag," insisted Holmes. "I heard it had bite marks on it."

"I don't give a monkey's what you've heard. I'm telling you it was Kane or one of his lot."

There was a silence at that, a clear sense that those around us had been shocked at the mere mention of the man's name.

Holmes let the awkwardness hang there for a moment before, with all pretence of innocence, saying, "Who's Kane then? Local lad is he?" Nobody saw fit to reply. "Only if he's got any work on offer I might be convinced to keep my feet on dry land for a while."

Someone reached out and took Holmes' drink from him.

"I'd get out while you still have legs to do so," said a dry, rasping voice.

"I didn't mean nothing," said the old man, but then shut his mouth once more as he decided silence was his best option for survival.

"Touchy lot, ain't you?" said Holmes. "Come on, Jim," he said and pushed his way towards the door. Realising he meant me, and needing little in the way of encouragement, I followed on.

CHAPTER TWELVE

"Well, that went well," I said with some sarcasm once we were back out on the street.

"I thought so," agreed Holmes, offering a smile that, when framed by his bald, tattooed face, looked positively terrifying.

"What did you hope to gain by that?" I asked. "Other than having to drink two pints of that foul muck they had the audacity to term 'ale.'"

Holmes suddenly stopped and yanked me to one side. To the side of the Bouquet of Lilies was a rough lean-to, a small covered area where the landlord kept a padlocked coal-house and a pile of logs. Holmes pushed me into the shadows just as a high-pitched whistling noise rang in my ears. I felt a cold rush of air go past my face as something flashed past and then came to a percussive stop in the upright post of the lean-to.

"Dear God!" I exclaimed, looking at the still-vibrating hilt of the dagger that had passed not a foot from my head. "That could have been the end of me!"

"Have patience," said Holmes. "They probably haven't finished yet."

"I can't see a thing," I admitted, staring out into the shadows.

"Luckily for us, neither can they."

Holmes plucked the knife free from the wood and looked at it. "Interesting," he said, "a German knife." He glanced at me. "We've had a lucky escape, the knife-throwers of Hamburg are incredibly accurate."

"I am struck dumb by relief," I muttered, somewhat exasperated by the way he was happy to show off, even while our lives were under threat.

We heard the sound of footsteps coming towards us. Holmes grabbed my arm and yanked me towards the street behind the pub. "Run!" he shouted. "Your life depends on it!"

Didn't it always?

CHAPTER THIRTEEN

We made our way through the backstreets, the sound of footsteps never far behind us. I didn't know if Holmes had a particular destination in mind. His passage seemed entirely random as we turned left, then right, then left again, weaving our way through the narrow passageways and terraces. More likely, I realised, he was trying to ensure that our pursuers never had a clear line of sight for long enough to throw another knife, like a soldier zigzagging before enemy fire in the hope of avoiding a bullet.

I was armed. Holmes may mock my willingness to risk the wrath of the law by carrying a loaded firearm on our excursions but I was damned if I was going to skulk around the roughest parts of Rotherhithe without some form of protection. It was little use to me at the moment anyway. I may have been a medical man more than a soldier but even I knew that in the time it took for me to turn around and find my aim I would likely have a knife in my chest. If we were able to find cover so that I could turn the tables then maybe we'd stand a fighting chance.

Breathlessly, I suggested as much to Holmes. But he just shook his head and continued to drag me through the backstreets of Rotherhithe.

We emerged close to the river again, having evidently looped right around. Holmes grabbed my arm and pulled me behind a stack of empty crates. I reached for my gun but he held down my hand and placed his fingers to his lips. Within a few moments our pursuers appeared. The first was as hairless as Holmes appeared to be, a thick scar running its way through his pale skin from the top of his head to the corner of his lips. The second made a pretence at refinement, his suit and glistening watch chain such an unfamiliar sight in this environment that it was a wonder he was able to walk the streets unmolested. Or perhaps that said all one needed to know about his potential for violence: only a man confident in his ability to take on all comers would have the audacity to dress in such a manner.

The man with the scar had a knife in his hand, the partner of the one that had narrowly missed us earlier. He spun it in his hand, letting blade revolve after hilt like a deadly carriage wheel.

"Lost them," said the dapper fellow.

"You give up too easily," said his scarred comrade, and I noted the German accent as predicted by Holmes. "They must be hiding close by."

"Probably." The other man was struggling to catch his breath. "But I'm in no mood to keep chasing them. I'm not paid to run around the docks all night."

"Lazy."

The dapper man fixed his comrade with a mean-spirited glare. "Keep a civil tongue, Klaus," he said. "I'm not beyond beating a bit of respect out of you should it be necessary."

Klaus smiled and, thanks to the scar, it twisted all of his features out of kilter. It was as if a painter had swept his hand across the face of a still-wet portrait. "You don't want to pick a fight with me, Martin, I'll cut your pretty face off."

"Like someone once tried to do to yours?"

"Oh no," said Klaus, running the tip of his knife along the thick ridge of his scar, "this was me. I get bored sometimes."

Martin shook his head. "The people I have to work with." He reached into his pocket and removed a silver cigarette case. Taking out a cigarette, he tapped it affectedly on the case, placed it between his lips and then replaced the case in his pocket. From a different pocket he removed a box of matches, lit the cigarette and exhaled a large, blue cloud of smoke. The whole business was so theatrical and affected, clearly designed to show Klaus how singularly unconcerned he was at the man's threats.

"Let's go and see Kane," he said after another draw on his cigarette. "We'll tell him that someone was asking after him."

"And admit we lost them?"

Martin shrugged. "I'm not ashamed of it. They obviously knew where they were going. He doesn't pay me to run around the streets all night."

"Fine. Then you will tell him who it was that decided they not bothered to find them." Klaus wore his accent like a badge, a brutal club to beat his grammar with.

Martin resorted to showmanship again, tossing his half-smoked cigarette at Klaus' feet before pushing past him and walking off along the quay. "All right then," he shouted back. "I will."

Klaus ground the cigarette beneath his boot with far more violence than the job warranted, and followed on behind.

Holmes waited a moment longer and then whispered in my ear.

"Now we have someone who can lead us to wherever this Kane fellow conducts his business," he said. "Far more useful than a pair of crooks with one of your bullets in them, don't you think?"

"Of course," I sighed. "If someone had seen fit to tell me what the plan was in the first place…"

"I've already told you," said Holmes, "no explanations, you can follow at your own pace."

He slipped out from behind the crates and began following Klaus and Martin, keeping to the shadows.

Restraining the urge to shoot him myself, I did likewise.

There was something to be said for Martin's insufferable ego – it made him an easy man to follow. He walked with confidence and swagger, never once feeling the need to check for others around him. He was the only important man in his world. He was an idiot. This fact was not lost on Klaus but he was clearly so angry at his colleague that he was also distracted from the path of common sense. Following them along the quayside was unproblematic, and when they came to the side door of a large warehouse, we hung back and watched as they stepped inside.

"It would appear Kane has a sizeable central office," I said, glancing up at the building. "For a new organisation, he's doing rather well."

"Isn't he," agreed Holmes.

According to the large, white letters painted on the side of the building, it belonged to E.C. Kenton & Waldemar, who offered "Animal Feed and Farming Supplies" – all suitably innocuous.

"Shall we?" asked Holmes, strolling up to the door.

I took my revolver out of my pocket and we made to step inside.

CHAPTER FOURTEEN

I pushed past Holmes into the doorway, determined that, if one of us should be poking his nose into the unknown, there should be a loaded firearm nearby in order to stop it being, as it were, cut off.

I could hear the retreating footsteps of Klaus and Martin, though it was so dark inside I could see nothing. There was a thick, sweet smell of grain and the ground underfoot was slightly sticky as we stepped inside and closed the door behind us.

Slowly our eyes grew accustomed to the darkness; the faint light offered through the skylights above was enough for us to get an idea of our surroundings. The open space of the warehouse was filled with stacked crates and sacks, row after row of them. Holmes climbed up the closest stack and burrowed beneath the tarpaulin. I heard him draw out a pocket knife and tear at the sack underneath. After a moment he reappeared.

"As far as I can tell," he explained, "it's nothing more than grain."

"Hardly criminal."

He looked around. "Who knows how much of this is just window-dressing?" he said. "Perhaps Messrs Kenton and Waldemar do indeed deal in animal food, with Kane working under their innocuous cover."

He jumped down and we made our way after Klaus and Martin.

Towards the rear of the warehouse, Holmes bid me to stop as he craned to listen. Just ahead of us there was a rattle of metal and the sound of something being dragged across the floor. We could hear rushing water, accompanied by the sound of Klaus and Martin struggling. Moving closer we saw them, lit by a lantern in Martin's hand, descending through a hole in the ground.

"I hate this," Martin moaned. "Why I can't work for someone who conducts business where it's dry and clean is beyond me. Have you seen the state of the walkway down there?" He looked up at Klaus. "What am I asking? You probably feel right at home."

Klaus nudged the man with his toe. "Keep with the talk pretty boy, I'll send you for a swim down there. Let you float to the river with the rest of the filth."

Martin paused in his climb down to stare back up at the German. "I have a feeling the two of us aren't going to work well together," he said. "I just can't imagine I won't end up killing you before the week is out."

"You make big promise," said Klaus, mangling his English more than ever.

Martin disappeared and, with a low growl like an irritated dog's, Klaus followed on after him.

"What charming fellows," muttered Holmes. "I might advise Kane that he would achieve a great deal more if he could only keep his staff in line."

"Seems to me he's doing all right," I said. "Though, on reflection, I would aspire to a lair located somewhere other than a sewer."

"Perfect place if you can tolerate the smell," Holmes replied. "A whole city could be hidden beneath our feet, with invisible access to all parts of the metropolis."

"All well and good until you die of cholera."

"Yes, Doctor." Holmes moved over to the grating which Klaus had slid back into place behind him. "I suggest we give them a few more moments to get clear," he said. "I am more than capable of following their trail after all. It wouldn't do to bump into them."

"Agreed." I would happily never come face to face with either gentleman again.

Holmes walked over to the closest row of crates and flipped back the tarpaulin. Looking around, he spied a crow bar, fetched it and loosened the crate's lid. He stepped back as the smell from inside assailed his nostrils.

"Some form of dried meat," he said, replacing the lid, "packed in strips."

"Animal food then. As claimed on the outside of the building."

He nodded, reached into his pockets and withdrew a box of matches. "Shall we go?" he asked, squatting down to lift the drain cover.

I helped him to lift it as noiselessly as possible. Klaus and Martin should have been some way ahead of us by now but the noise would carry down there, and we didn't want to announce our presence. We stood listening for a moment. Faintly we could hear the sound of talking, presumably the two thugs. It was clearly coming from some distance away. Holmes lit a match and dropped it through the hole. Briefly it illuminated a short ladder leading to a narrow walkway. "It would be wisest to use light sparingly," he whispered.

"To begin with, let us follow the evidence of our ears and be careful where we place our feet."

"Very careful," I agreed, disgusted at the thought of traversing the sewer network in the dark. The pair of us descended.

I was about to draw the cover back into place when Holmes stopped me. "The sound of you dragging that will travel some way down here," he said. "We'll risk leaving it."

I nodded, then realised he couldn't see me, not that it mattered. I could tell he had already begun to move along the walkway.

Moving as carefully and quietly as I could, I followed Holmes. The sound of voices continued ahead of us. I couldn't make out the words but the tone clearly marked the speakers as Klaus and Martin.

We walked for some time and I tried to imagine where our route was taking us above ground. My knowledge of the city south of the river was not good and, while I could tell that we must be some way beyond the docks of Rotherhithe by now, I could say no more. No doubt Holmes could have recited the street and house number but, naturally, he was still sticking to his childish silence.

After a while, other voices joined those of Klaus and Martin. Clearly we were approaching the hub of Kane's hideout.

Light began to filter towards us, though a curve in the tunnel kept its source hidden. Holmes held out his arm and we advanced the last few feet with extra caution. The last thing we wanted to do was suddenly reveal ourselves in a flood of light.

There was a general bout of raucous welcome as Klaus and Martin were greeted by their comrades. I tried to count how many people were gathered there by discerning their different voices, and decided there were seven or eight – hardly a large gang but more than enough to see us hopelessly outnumbered if our presence was spotted.

Holmes slipped his head around the bend in the tunnel then pressed his lips close to my ear. "We should have a few more feet of darkness to conceal us," he said. "Tread carefully and keep that gun of yours handy."

I hardly needed encouraging on either point.

We turned the corner and moved one careful foot at a time, Holmes keeping his eye on where the light fell, judging how close we could get and still remain in shadow were they to look towards us.

The open space was a veritable cathedral of old brick, a central atrium with alcoves around its towering walls. A series of jetties served a central platform. This platform was laid out with tables and chairs, packing crates, other assorted furniture, and provisions – enough for a working camp. The lights were provided by gas lamps strung in diagonal rows across the whole structure. I knew that such impressive sights lay beneath London – feats of engineering both modern and as ancient as the Roman occupation of the city – but I had never imagined they could have been turned to such a purpose.

A pair of narrow gondolas was moored alongside a jetty by way of transport. No doubt the gang could travel the entire length and breadth of the city without ever having to come up into the fresh air.

My rough guess had been accurate – there were five other gang members with Klaus and Martin, bringing the total up to seven.

"Where's Kane?" Martin asked, dropping into a chair on the central platform.

One of the others, older than the rest, sporting a genuine version of the white hair and beard I was affecting, took a nostril full of snuff and replied, in a nasal tone of voice, "Out on one of the boats, ain't he?"

"Gone fishing!" another shouted.

"Even he wouldn't eat what comes out of that water," a third added. "Most of it's been eaten once already!"

There was a roar of laughter at that.

Klaus took a seat across the room from Martin. "There is someone who is asking questions," he said. "We made chase but Martin does not like to run."

"Crumples his strides, don't it?" said another in a thick Geordie accent.

"Wears out his expensive shoe leather!" the lavatorial wit from earlier added.

"Couldn't see the point," Martin insisted. "They weren't important, probably just after work."

"Who wants work?" asked a deep voice. Another gondola appeared from an opposite tunnel. The man inside it had to stoop so as not to lose his hat on the low ceiling. Once out in the open he gained his full height. There was a great deal of it – the man was a veritable giant. His face was covered with a long black net hanging from the brim of his hat that made him look like a beekeeper. He wore a large black overcoat and his large hands were hidden inside shining leather mittens. As he approached the central platform, the effect was that of an overwhelming shadow looming across the water.

"Pair of blokes drinking in the Bucket of Lies, Boss," answered Martin. "Asking a load of questions about the floaters."

"Floaters?"

"The bodies, Boss, wanting to know all about it."

Kane, for there could be little doubt that's who it was, reached the jetty where the other vessels were moored and stepped up out of the gondola. He tied it up and walked towards the rest of them, his heavy footsteps echoing around the chamber.

"Police?" he asked.

"No," Klaus replied, no doubt wanting to make it clear to his employer that he had also been present. "You can tell when it is the policemen dressed up."

"They're like cheap music hall," the Geordie said. "All false moustaches and braces."

There was another bout of laughter at that, with the Geordie prancing around like a cheap theatre act.

"If you could restrain yourself for once, Campbell," Kane said, "we might get to the truth sooner."

"Sorry, Boss," Campbell replied. "Never can resist a laugh."

"Well, try," his employer insisted. That huge, veiled head turned towards Martin. "Tell me."

Martin shifted in his seat, the arrogance and bravado he had displayed earlier now gone. "Klaus and I were having a drink when this pair of blokes came in and started talking…"

"Describe them."

"One had a shaven head, all inks and scars, you know. An ocean-going feller so he said, and he looked the part. His mate was the spit of Jackson here." He pointed at the older man, who was scratching away at his long beard.

"They said they came from the *Spirit of Mayfair*," said Klaus.

Kane turned towards the German. "And did you believe them?"

Klaus hesitated for a moment, wanting to give a truthful answer. "Yes," he said, "I believed them."

Kane nodded, and turned back to Martin.

"So they were asking about the bodies?"

"Yeah," Martin agreed. "You know, wanting to know all the grisly details. The shaved one seemed to think it must have been an animal what done it."

"He said that?" asked Kane. "Not gangs?"

"We know no gang would have done it, Boss," said the old man.

"*We* know that, Jackson, but I am interested as to whether they did."

"Well, that's what they said," confirmed Martin. "Though they sounded as thick as this water to be honest."

"I would trust you to perform many tasks," said Kane, "but not to judge the intelligence of others. Why did you say they were looking for work?"

"They mentioned your name," Klaus said.

"Only after someone else did," insisted Martin. "The old bloke who was doing all the talking, he said it first."

Kane looked to Klaus. "Did he?"

Klaus shrugged. "I do not remember. But I thought we should question them about it…"

"We followed them for a bit," Martin interrupted. "But they knew their way around and gave us the slip."

"They knew you were following?"

"He tried to put one of his knives in them, so they weren't in much doubt."

Kane walked over to Klaus, towering over the man. "You tried to kill them?"

"No," Klaus' voice trembled. He had expected Martin to be on the receiving end of Kane's irritation, not himself. "Just slow them down."

"Slow them down?" Kane shook his head, its massive, shapeless form casting a shadow across the wall. "I imagine a knife in the back would do that, yes."

"What do you care, anyway?" Klaus asked, becoming even more defensive. "So what if I do kill some worthless navy trash?"

"You kill when I tell you to kill," Kane replied. "Because you work for me. People who work for me do as they're told."

"All right," Klaus said, holding up his hands. "I understand."

"Do you?" Kane asked. "Do you understand completely?" He reached out and took Klaus' hands, pinching them between the shiny black pincers of his leather mittens. "Because you like working for me, don't you?"

"Yes! Yes!" Klaus tried to pull his hands away but Kane held them firmly.

"Good," Kane said. "Then I will not hurt your knife-throwing hand." There was a cracking noise as Kane crushed the fingers of Klaus' left hand. He barely seemed to move, as if all he needed to do was squeeze. Whatever the reason for those strange mittens, they concealed powerful hands.

I drew a breath, suppressing my distaste and fear. It was the tiniest noise, much too quiet to carry as far as the platform. Nonetheless, Kane turned towards us, inclining his head as if craning to listen. The light of the lantern fell behind Kane's hooded head for a moment and I caught sight of its shape beneath the black netting. It was utterly deformed, elongated and protruding in all the wrong places. No wonder he chose to keep it hidden. Just a glimpse of it had been enough to send a shiver down my spine. If that hadn't done so then his next words certainly would have done:

"We are being watched!" he said, twisting that deformed head again, this time in the other direction. I was reminded of a pigeon inclining itself from one side to the other. He inhaled sharply before pointing directly towards us. "There!" he shouted. "Two of them!"

"Holmes," I said, "run! I shall get us a head start."

So saying, I raised my revolver and loosed two rounds. I am not a bad shot, despite the fact that my army career was dedicated to saving lives rather than taking them. Though I freely admit the fact that I hit both of the lanterns I was aiming for was lucky. They ejected their flaming oil in a spray over the heads of Kane's gang, offering a perfect distraction as we turned into the darkness and began to run.

Those first few steps were disorientating: blinded from the flash of light that had accompanied the exploding lantern, I found the darkness all the more impenetrable as I followed Holmes. Keeping my elbow against the bricks to my left, I used the wall to guide me, rather than my eyes. We needed to be quick but also sure-footed. If we stumbled off the path and into the water then they would catch us for sure.

Behind us the sound of panicked shouts began to coalesce into something more purposeful. Kane's gang had presumably extinguished the small fires I had caused and were now preparing to follow. As I listened, I heard the noises of something closer – a laboured, snarling breathing and the heavy fall of booted feet. I imagined Kane himself, forcing his large bulk along the narrow pathway, determined not to let us slip away from him. The noises drew closer and closer. There was no sign of light from a lantern, so I could only assume he was as blind as we were. It seemed to cause him less discomfort. Closer and closer came the sound of his boots, heavy leather soles beating at the wet brick. Each footfall boasted of his size and weight, a giant's tread. I had seen how easily he had snapped bone between his fingers – were those grotesque leather mittens even now reaching out for me? I could swear that laboured breathing was mere feet away now, so close as to almost dampen the back of my neck.

I turned and fired blindly into the darkness. In the muzzle flash I caught a terrifying glimpse of Kane who was indeed almost within reach. His hat and veil had come loose and the face that leered at me in that sudden moment of illumination was a dark, terrible thing of teeth and pink maw. The image was so brief as to be impossible to fix, though it clung to me even as I heard him splash into the water – whether darting for cover, or because I actually hit him, I could not say. I turned back to keep running but with every step I saw that terrible face. What kind of wound could have exposed so much of his mouth? As if the cheeks had been split wide either side so his head could hinge by those monstrous teeth. Whatever had caused his deformity, I could understand only too well his desire to hide it.

"Watson!" Holmes shouted.

"I'm fine," I replied. "How much farther?"

For a moment my foot grazed the edge of the path and I came close to losing my balance and tumbling into the sewer water alongside. I held my hand out to steady myself.

"Just keep running!" Holmes replied.

Kane was splashing in the water, presumably pulling himself back out to continue the chase. As I listened further, I realised he was actually swimming, his gang heading after us on foot. As he continued to pull himself through the water with those powerful arms I ran after Holmes, hoping that he would find escape soon.

Surely we didn't have to exit by the same manhole we entered? Wouldn't anywhere do at this point?

He seemed to answer my thoughts, his hand darting out of the darkness and grabbing me by the lapel as I made to run past.

"This way," he said, tugging me upwards where it now became clear that a ladder was mounted to take us towards street level.

I climbed as fast as I could. Which, with the sounds of pursuit still all too close, was fast indeed. There was a clatter above my head as the steel cover was lifted and pushed aside.

"Quickly man!" came Holmes' voice.

As I felt the cool air of the world above hit my face, I was aware of the ladder shaking beneath me. Someone else – and it could be only Kane – had begun to climb.

"Right behind me," I said as I pulled myself out onto the road surface. I hadn't exaggerated either. The ladder had been shaken violently enough that it would surely soon come loose from its fastenings.

"Move!" Holmes cried, standing over the hole and placing what looked like a small blowpipe to his lips. He blew and the most awful roar of pain echoed up from beneath the street. A second later this was followed by a loud splash; Kane had clearly fallen back into the water.

"Dear Lord!" I cried. "What did you shoot him with?"

"No explanations," Holmes replied, infuriatingly, dragging the manhole cover back into place and dropping the pipe into his pocket. "Now, might I suggest we find a cab to take us to safe territory before the rest of his gang are on our heels?"

PART TWO

FEAR THE LAW

CHAPTER FIFTEEN

Find a cab? Naturally that was a far-from-simple task. Two gentlemen, dressed as vagrants and fresh – or quite the opposite – from the sewer will find it hard to befriend cab drivers. It was only by my holding up a pound note and agreeing a grotesquely inflated price upfront that I managed to secure us transport.

Once back at Baker Street, Holmes went straight to his room, leaving me to wash and struggle my way clear of my disguise. The damnable thing was cemented to my skin, and it was sore-faced and pink as a lobster that I finally settled down to sleep.

It may surprise some of my readers that I was even able to do such a thing but I can only say that, working with Holmes, you learned to take the terrifying in your stride. You also learned to take your sleep where you could find it; he was certainly not beyond waking you up before the dawn demanding you accompany him on one errand or another.

* * *

Thankfully that was not to be the case the next morning. I breakfasted alone, Holmes already having vanished, much to Mrs Hudson's irritation. She never did like to see her food go to waste, a fate I assured her I would help it to avoid, having woken with the hunger of an ox.

Thus, working my way through two plates of bacon, eggs and kidneys, I resolved to spend the morning putting the peace and quiet to good use: I would dedicate my thoughts to the case. I know such an announcement is likely to create amusement amongst a number of my readers – I have received enough letters damning my faculties to know what the greater reading public thinks of my deductive abilities – but Holmes' churlishness had put me in a competitive mood, and I was determined to prove my worth. In my defence, I will also point out that a perfectly serviceable candle may struggle to impress when placed next to a large gas lamp; in comparing my powers of deduction to those of Holmes, mine will always be found wanting.

Bearing all this in mind, I was nonetheless determined to make a dent in the case.

Once the breakfast plates were cleared, I asked Mrs Hudson for more coffee and set about making some notes, all the better to organise what we knew already. I shall spare the reader the inconvenience of ploughing through all of them verbatim, but shall nonetheless attempt to lay out the main points regarding the cadavers:

Body number-one – Male. Washed up and rapidly disposed of, not thought to be anything more than an accident. Information limited.

Body number-two – Male. Discovered by a gang of children.

Manacled hands and feet. Signs of considerable abuse prior to death. Body had been beaten. (Interrogation, perhaps?) Investigating police surgeon believed he recognised both tiger- and snake-bites. (Indian connection?) The body was dead by the time it was dumped in the water. This can be deduced from the fact that there was no water in the lungs.

Body number-three – Male. In an even worse state than the previous cadavers – more of a collection of parts than an intact body. The tooth marks around a wound on what remained of the torso identified the attacking creature as a shark most often found in Australian waters. Given the state of the remains, it is impossible to tell whether it had been treated in a similar manner to the second.

Accepting those facts, we had Shinwell Johnson's insistence that the bodies were not, as was speculated in the press, the result of gang violence. His logic for this was that you only committed such theatrical killings if you were sending a message, and if you were sending a message you signed your name to it. The thinking was sound enough and further endorsed by the snatch of conversation we had heard in the tunnels. "We know no gang could have done it," Martin had announced, and Kane had agreed with him. Though whether that could be taken as actual fact rather than a sign they shared the same opinion as Johnson, it was impossible to say. Kane and his gang didn't believe the murders were committed by gangs – that is all we could say for sure.

So, what could we say with regard to motive? The second body showed clear signs of having been interrogated, so the perpetrator was after information. Of what sort we could not say.

I was, by this point, realising there was a great deal we could not say! And what of Moreau? What evidence did we even have that he was involved?

Aside from the death of Prendick and the fact that these bodies showed signs of attack from exotic animals, there was absolutely none. Could it be that Mycroft had been withholding information? It seemed unlikely he was basing his fears on those two facts alone.

Prendick.

I underlined that name and then added two others: *Montgomery* and *Moreau.* I decided that procrastinating over paper was all very well, but we needed more information, and that was unlikely simply to fall into our hands.

I would find out all I could about the three men capable of reproducing these experiments.

CHAPTER SIXTEEN

I started my investigations by inquiring after Mycroft. Needless to say he was not receiving visitors. Locked away within the book-lined walls of the Diogenes Club, he frequently instructed the staff to fend off all callers. He talked to the world only when he wished it.

With that method of inquiry closed, I decided to call on Norman Greenhough, my editor at *The Strand*. This was something I tried to avoid wherever possible, as Norman's pursuit of material often bordered on the vicious. That day was no exception.

"John!" he called, reaching inside the liquor cabinet he concealed behind a counterfeit row of books on his shelf. "How nice to see you. Care for a drink?"

"Bit early for me," I admitted, having never adapted to the liquid consumption of those who worked in publishing.

He checked his watch, white moustache twitching. "You may have a point there," he admitted. "I've been in the office since yesterday and one loses track."

He walked to his door, opened it and bellowed for his secretary to find some morning coffee and something that might pass for an ad hoc breakfast.

"Why so late?" I asked as he settled back down behind his desk.

"Oh the usual crackpots and loons," he said. "We've had a reader threaten to blow the place up unless we reveal the whereabouts of Raffles."

"Raffles?"

"You know, Hornung's character – gentleman thief, homosexual and anti-Semite – the character, not the man. I don't think so anyway…"

"Oh yes, him." I might add that Norman's opinion of the character's attributes were not necessarily shared by his creator. The editor was famed for his jocular dismissal of most of the work he published. I had no doubt that, were Ernest Hornung to pop in for a chat about his latest submission, Norman would moan for a few minutes about "that upstart medico and his smart-aleck room-mate". "And why do they feel such a need for an amateur cracksman?"

"Who knows? And it doesn't matter how many times you insist the only place Raffles can be found is in the flaccid forebrain of his creator, the fools won't listen. Some people just can't help but blur the lines between fiction and reality."

"Have you alerted the police?"

"Heavens, no. If they could really build a bomb they could surely blow up their own safe. If they turn up at the office I'll have a couple of the print boys throw them out on their ear. It just sends everything into a panic for a few days. Nothing scares the filing clerks like a bomb threat, and before you know it half the staff are claiming to be trapped in their sick beds." He mopped his brow with the florid silk handkerchief he kept stuffed in his jacket pocket. "Lily-livered lot! Oh, for a decent war! They could use the training."

Not being altogether able to recommend the experience of combat, I decided to try and change the subject.

"I wanted to talk to you about a series of press articles I remember from a few years ago," I said.

"Oh," he replied. "I rather hoped you were planning to offer me a novel."

"Just short stories at the moment I'm afraid," I said. "I haven't the time for a full-length piece."

"But the public love the serials," he insisted. "They queue up around the block."

"I'm afraid most of our cases just don't really suit the format."

"Couldn't they be...well, padded out a bit?"

"I'd rather not."

"You know – a few red herrings, trips to the country. Throw in another moor and they'll be biting our hands off – they were as rabid as the damned dog during our serialisation of the Baskerville case!"

"I understand that, Norman," I said. "But I really can only work with the case files I have. Besides, I think the stories read much better when they're kept trim."

"Our bank disagrees. What are you working on at the moment? Following up that business with the chef?"

"Chef?"

"Andre Le Croix. Famous chap, fat, did a runner on the opening night of his new restaurant."

"Not really our sort of thing."

"No, I suppose not. Shame though, I was one of the diners and the whole night put me out a couple of quid. You sure I couldn't get you to hunt him down for me?"

"I'm not your personal debt-collection service, Norman. I'm afraid the current case is not for publication."

"Top secret, eh?" he asked, a vicious glint in his eye.

The last thing I wanted to do was encourage him. "Not at all, it just wouldn't make a very good story. Now, about these articles…"

Which was when the coffee arrived, and my request was curtailed by the serving of drinks. I fielded the offer of sandwiches.

Finally, while Norman's mouth was filled with salmon paste, I tried to get the information I was after.

"Dr Moreau," I said. "Disgraced physiologist. Who was the reporter that broke the story?"

Norman swallowed, somewhat reluctantly. "What do you want to bring that lunatic up for?" he asked. "Thinking about him's likely to put me right off my sandwiches."

I apologised, and waffled about researching for a science-fiction story.

"Science fiction?" he asked, poking uncertainly at the indeterminate filling of another sandwich with the nib of his pen. "What do you want to write that sort of rubbish for? Grisly murders and heaving bosoms, that's what the readers want." He popped the sandwich into his mouth. "Come to think of it, I wouldn't mind a bit of both myself."

"I may not even want to publish," I insisted. "But you know what it's like when you have an idea – you just have to follow where the muse takes you…" This was unutterable guff but Norman swallowed it as easily as his ad hoc breakfast.

"Fella's name was Mitchell," he said. "He was a freelancer. Believe it or not I've published him myself. Though keep it under your hat – the three or four old pussies who write demanding to know who authored 'The Adventures of Professor Q' have been informed it's a state secret." He winked over the rim of his coffee cup as he took a big mouthful. "That sort of nonsense sells copies. I can give you his address if you like."

"If you're sure he wouldn't mind?"

"My dear Doctor, you don't know writers like I do – he'll be over the moon to have such a famous personage on his doormat. I give it five minutes before he's trying to convince you to co-write a novel with him!"

CHAPTER SEVENTEEN

In actuality, the subject of co-writing a novel never came up. But then Mitchell clearly had other things on his mind. He spent the first five minutes convincing himself I wasn't a spy for the Russian monarchy – it would seem he had been writing a piece on them that had ruffled some Tsarist feathers. Eventually it was my mentioning Mycroft that finally calmed him down.

"That's a name that rarely brings good news," he said, "though at least he was never boring."

Sentiments mirrored by Sherlock, I noted.

"I haven't heard from him for years. I did him a small favour once – brought certain matters to a head in order to serve his purpose." He smiled. "We all have to do our bit for Queen and country after all."

Rather than spin a similar tale to the one I had offered Norman Greenhough, I simply explained to Mitchell that I wanted to know everything he could tell me about Moreau. I gave no reason but equally offered no excuse. Given that he had worked with Mycroft in the matter, I saw no need to be circumspect. He laughed, which had certainly not been the response I was expecting.

"I can tell Mycroft hasn't sent you now," he said, "he would never countenance such straight talking! The man's a veritable oyster when it comes to information. I suppose you must be *the* John Watson?"

I admitted as much. The stress on the definite article always made me feel bizarrely embarrassed – it was something I was asked rather a lot. I had never grown used to the notion that I was deemed to be famous by the general public. But then, most famous people probably never do. They see themselves from the inside and therefore know they are the very epitome of normality and drudgery.

"I suppose therefore –" he smiled "– I'm a writer. You must forgive me but we do a lot of supposing – that you're involved in an investigation with Mr Sherlock Holmes?"

Once again I admitted he was right, but still chose not to elaborate.

"You're going to make me keep guessing, aren't you Doctor?" he smiled.

"Isn't that what journalists excel at?" I replied, returning his smile.

"I suppose it is." He took a cigarette from a small case he kept in his jacket pocket and offered one to me. Realising I would be better off trying to get along with the man than continually rebut him, I took one and we smoked for a minute while he ransacked his shelves.

"That was a fascinating period," he said, sucking contemplatively on his cigarette. "Terrifying of course, but Moreau was quite the most fascinating man I had ever met."

"And surely one of the most reprehensible?"

"Oh yes –" he smiled "– that too. But then I spend a great deal of my time in the company of truly loathsome human beings. Most of the work I've done has been getting under the skin of the real monsters in our society."

"I suppose I could say the same, Holmes certainly could."

"And are you digging away beneath just such a surface now?"

I realised I couldn't expect him to offer me much unless I showed myself to be at least partially willing to share.

"Our current investigation overlaps with the work of Moreau," I said. "He casts a long shadow and it would be extremely useful were we to be able to understand him a little better."

"Understand him? Oh I doubt you'll ever do that. He was quite beyond such a thing as comprehension. I simply followed in his wake and tried to conceive of his goals. Of course, at the time, it was by no means certain he actually had any. He talked big, naturally. All scientists do in my experience – they all intend to make us live forever or crack the Earth open like an egg. Still, I found it hard to believe that the things he did within that laboratory had a viable goal. Back then, of course, I had very little scientific knowledge at all, so it's hardly surprising that his work was beyond me. From what I heard later it seems likely that he wasn't quite as pointlessly mad as most people originally thought."

"Where did you hear about his later work?" I was by no means certain that he should know of such things, though if he had worked with Mycroft I dare say he was privy to more information than most.

"You hear most things in my line of work, Doctor," he said, "especially when you've been doing it for as long as I have. I heard all about Edward Prendick and his story of having met Moreau in the South Pacific, about the creatures he met there..."

"And did you believe any of it?"

"I can honestly say I would be willing to believe anything with regards Moreau, he was an extremely capable monster." He suddenly jumped up from his seat. "I kept all of my notes from the time I spent working with him," he said, moving over to his desk and picking up a large folder. "They're not pleasant reading but you're welcome to borrow them should they be useful."

"You're too kind." This was more than I had hoped for.

"No, it comes with a price – would you keep me informed? I know you can't tell me everything, but I would appreciate being involved as much as you can allow. After all, it wouldn't be the first time I'd worked with the government!"

I was by no means sure this was a deal I could afford to accept, but the opportunity to take his notes was a hard one to turn down.

"As soon as I can reveal more," I said, "I will. I'll even ask Mycroft if you can be put in the picture. How would that be?"

At the mention of Mycroft his face soured a little. "Perhaps it would be better not to appeal to him," he said. "I've found myself somewhat at odds with him in recent years."

"He can be a hard gentleman to get on with."

Mitchell nodded. "And I often find myself in, shall we say, legally complex positions." He grinned at his phraseology. "As a journalist you sometimes have to tread delicately to get the story you want. I've done nothing that I'm ashamed of, I hasten to add, but I can understand why Mycroft felt it necessary to distance himself from me. He does have to maintain a whiter-than-white reputation."

He handed the file over. "Never mind, tell me what you can when you can, I'll settle for that. If there's a story in it down the line I'd like to be ahead of the game."

"Understood."

CHAPTER EIGHTEEN

I left Mitchell's home with the bundle of notes beneath my arm, and ruminated upon whether to return to Baker Street or continue fishing for information. The thought of Holmes' insufferable arrogance decided me. Instead of making my way home I called in at Scotland Yard.

"Doctor!" Lestrade was apparently pleased to see me, which brought to mind Holmes' statements from the night before. Did the policeman truly resent the impression I had created of him in the popular press? I decided simply to ask him outright, and to Hell with it. He stared at me for a moment, clearly surprised by the question. Then he laughed.

"I don't think I've had to pay for a single beer in the last twelve years, Doctor," he said, "which is more than enough compensation for any slights on my professional ability." He took a big mouthful from a cup of tea on his desk. "There's not a copper from here to Glasgow that doesn't want to hear a story or two. 'Is 'e really like 'e seems in the magazines?' they ask. 'Can 'e really do those tricksy little numbers where he guesses all about a person from the way they comb their hair or knot their tie?' The questions are never-ending."

"That alone must get somewhat tiresome," I suggested.

"Nah…" Lestrade dumped his teacup back on the desk, where its dregs splashed onto a stack of crime reports. It made me think of bloodstains. Perhaps I was spending altogether too much time with Holmes – everywhere I looked I imagined murder. "To be honest," Lestrade continued, "the attention's nice really. You don't get much credit in this job. You're someone to spit on or lob a brick at. More often than not when I say my name people want to shake my hand, not punch me. I doubt it's done me much harm with the powers that be, either."

"So, everything considered, I should be asking for a commission rather than apologising?"

He laughed. "There's no spare from my wage, Doctor! That's not changed, whatever else has!" He sat up straight, perhaps reminded by discussion of his salary that he had a job to do. "Surely you didn't come over here just to ask me about that, though?"

I admitted as much. "I was wondering if you could get me information on the death of a man called Edward Prendick. He lived somewhere rural and was believed to have committed suicide by drinking acid."

"'Lived somewhere rural'?" Lestrade laughed. "Don't believe in making things easy for me, do you?"

"Sorry, I had hoped to be able to narrow it down further."

"Actually you might be in luck, the name rings a bell." He got up and stuck his head out of the door of his office. "Oi!" he shouted. "Albert, 'as George left yet?"

A distant voice echoed back. "Only just – 'ang on a tick!"

There was a pause and the distant sound of shouting. After a few moments, a familiar, bespectacled face popped its head around the door.

"You wanted me?" asked Inspector Mann, a detective Holmes and I had met recently when investigating the grotesque death of Lord Ruthvney. He was wrapped in several layers against the cold, making him appear to waddle slightly as he entered the room. On noticing me, he laughed, shuffled over and shook my hand. "Well if it isn't Dr Watson," he said, "the man partially responsible for the most incomprehensible police statement I've ever had to write."

"Yes, I imagine it took some imaginative filing."

"Indeed it did. It's all very well for Mr Holmes – he doesn't have to bundle his deductions up into carefully constructed paragraphs and lists."

"He leaves that to me," I replied.

"Well, next time we cross paths perhaps you could be so good as to hand over the relevant issue of *The Strand* and I'll just file that."

He looked to Lestrade and put his hands in his pockets. "Might this be just such an occasion?"

"Indeed it might," I admitted, "if you know anything about the death of Edward Prendick."

He smiled. "Can I not have a single bizarre death on my patch without you two getting involved?" He pushed his glasses up his nose. "Do you want the quick version or the full tour? I was just heading back there and you're welcome to join me if you have the time and inclination."

I thought about it for a moment and decided the latter was definitely the way to go. If I was determined to gather evidence to rival Holmes then I needed to do it as per his methods and visit the actual scene of the crime.

"I'm game for a trip to the country!" I replied.

"Fine luck for some," said Lestrade.

CHAPTER NINETEEN

Mann and I made our way to Liverpool Street Station and boarded the one o'clock train to Billericay.

En route, Mann entertained me with stories of his country career. It was clear that he hankered for the crimes of the city despite the fact that he couldn't bear the thought of living there. "One must choose to cater for the soul or the brain," he said. "The former is never happier than when surrounded by green, but the latter begins to fossilise."

He kindly insisted on sharing his sandwiches – there was no dining car on such a local service of course – and it was an enjoyable journey, watching the buildings give way to fields as we munched on tongue and chutney.

On arrival at Billericay, Mann led me to the police station, a small building just off the main high street.

It was a charming little place and I could see why Mann was comfortable there. Still, having becoming utterly converted to city life I think I would have become bored of "Mrs Wilkinson's Tea Shoppe" and the company of the tweedy old squires seen through the window of the Dog and Sheep.

The station contained a small, open-front office manned by a large officer whose lustrous sideboards made him appear positively ovine.

"Afternoon, Sir," he said. "Fine time in the city was it?"

Mann smiled at me. "To Constable Scott, London is a mythical place, a foreign land."

"They certainly do things differently there," Scott agreed. "I can't say as I've ever fathomed what people see in it."

You would have thought Billericay was a remote Scottish island, not a market town a stone's throw from the capital.

Mann led me through to his office, which was filled floor to ceiling with well-stocked bookcases. I glanced along the shelves and saw everything from military history to gothic romances.

"I like to read," he admitted, "and the missus says I can't clutter the place up at home."

"Married life, eh?" I said with a smile, falling into the usual male banter.

"Ah," he said. "So there is a Mrs Watson then, eh?"

"There was," I replied, feeling suddenly awkward, as all widowers do. People don't like to hear about loss, they rarely know how to respond to it.

Mann handled it better than some. "Sorry to hear that," he said with a smile. "You always think you know the people you read about, of course you only know the half of people's lives."

"The half they choose to tell you."

"Indeed."

Sensing that the best way forward was to move on, he reached for a folder of notes that sat in the tray on his desk. "On the matter of Edward Prendick, perhaps it's better if I walk you through the affair. I have my notes here, for whatever help they may offer, and I still have a key to his house courtesy of the dead man's solicitor." He took the latter from a drawer in his desk and dropped it into his overcoat pocket. The folder of notes under his arm, he gestured to the door. "No sooner are we arrived than we head off again," he smiled. "It's a short walk to the house but I can give you the background on the way."

It was important, I felt, that we had one thing clear above all others:

"Is there any chance that the body found was not that of Edward Prendick?" I asked. "Had the acid disfigured enough to disguise his identity?"

"It did considerable damage of course," Mann agreed, "but the face was clear enough. The man we carried out of here was certainly Edward Prendick."

Which meant that the list of those theoretically able to replicate Moreau's work was most definitely reduced to two, the man himself and his assistant Montgomery, both of whom were supposed to have died on the island but we would never know for sure, not now that the one and only eyewitness was confirmed dead.

I had been sure that an investigation into Prendick's death would reveal flaws, a big enough crack that the man himself could have slipped through it. I trusted Mann's work, though, he was astute enough; if he said Prendick was dead then I had little doubt that was so. But was it suicide or murder?

We headed back out onto the high street, the sweetness of the shop windows, the fragile, lacy appearance of a town built on grace and gentility, not matched by Inspector Mann's conversation.

"Edward Prendick," he said, skirting past the doorway of a fishmonger and avoiding an ejected bucketful of crushed ice, "was known to the few locals that had cause to know him at all as George Herbert. He wished to keep his identity a secret and, having been frequently quoted in the press around the time of his rescue, he felt it best to maintain a pseudonym. It wasn't difficult given that he barely interacted with anyone from the town. If a man says his name's Herbert who has cause to disagree?"

We turned off the main street and began to walk towards the church.

"Every town has its reclusive citizens," Mann continued. "The rural life appeals to many different personalities but there will always be those who choose to live somewhere simply because it's a place where others aren't."

Looking at the hustle and bustle of the streets, I couldn't help but feel Mann was exaggerating. As someone who had spent time on Dartmoor I knew real wilderness when I had cause to be stuck in it.

"Of course," he said, as if predicting such an argument, "Billericay itself is a positive circus of activity, but some of the small villages that fall within my purview are empty places indeed – collections of houses with silent, unfriendly people in them. All staring out of the windows at one another and refusing to make conversation." He grinned. "Luckily they're mostly so shy they don't bump each other off either!"

Past the church was a narrow track that led out into the surrounding fields.

"Prendick had the best of both worlds as you'll see. He bought Moon Cottage some years ago, an old farmhouse with absolutely nobody on his doorstep. He had nothing around him but fields."

And very pleasant fields they were too, I thought, as we marched across them.

"Only two people dealt with him on a regular basis," said Mann. "Mrs Alice Bradley who worked as a home help, cleaning up a bit twice a week and Harold Court, the local postmaster."

"He received a lot of post?"

"Indeed, chemicals, equipment, specialist items. A lot of it needed to be signed for. Which is why Court was in a position to identify the body – he knew him well enough."

"Had he received any post on the day he died?"

"Hard to say for sure. Bear in mind the body wasn't discovered for some time and it was difficult to be precise as to the time of death. Normally, Mrs Bradley visits on a Tuesday and a Thursday. That week she was visiting her sister in Northampton and so Prendick would have had no visitors for ten days. We know he collected a parcel from Mr Court on the Wednesday. Mrs Bradley visited the following Thursday and found him dead. The local coroner – who's a good man, though I know we country folk are assumed lacking by the powers that be in the metropolis…"

"Not by me," I insisted.

He smiled. "Well, he claims Prendick could have died on the Wednesday but he wouldn't want to guarantee it either side of twenty-four hours or so."

We were clearing the crest of a hill and I could see a small cottage in the distance, still a good few minutes' walk away.

"Moon Cottage?" I asked.

"The very same," Mann agreed, leading us down the following slope.

"You're wondering," he continued, "whether Prendick received anything by the post that could have driven him to suicide."

"A man must have some encouragement to consider self-destruction."

"Indeed he must. But remember that Prendick may already have had it. He chose this life of solitude because he feared the world and everything he found in it. That was clear enough from the report he wrote of his rescue. He was a man who had faced the most unforgiving ridicule, in fact there had been talk of his being committed."

"He was already deeply damaged."

"Indeed. Which is why, as grotesque as it might seem, I am inclined to agree with the court's ruling that it was suicide."

We had almost reached the house by now and Mann drew to a halt to elaborate his point. "I agree that acid is an agonising choice of weapon, but Prendick showed considerable signs of mania as you'll soon see. Such people often choose to inflict great pain on themselves, a spiritual purging of some deluded sort." He counted the points off on the fingers of his gloved hand. "Add to that the fact that the place was locked up securely from the inside; we had to put a window through to get in."

"That could have been done simply to mislead?"

"Locked-room mysteries are all very well in fiction, Doctor, but they're not usual in the real world. Besides, it would have been a pointless effort in this case as we would have been inclined towards suicide anyway. The state of the walls – well, you'll see that in a minute. Finally, drinking acid may be vicious but it's hard to force someone else to do it. You haven't the benefit of seeing the body but it was ingested cleanly. If someone forced it down him one would expect signs of splashing, burn marks to the face and lips. As it is the damage was consistent with his drinking it calmly and slowly, incredible in itself given that it must have hurt from the moment it hit his palate."

"Another sign of mania perhaps," I said. "It's amazing what the human body can achieve when the mind is damaged. I've seen poor, deranged people commit the most terrible acts of self-mutilation and be almost completely unaware."

"My thoughts exactly." We walked the last few steps to the house and Mann removed the key from the pocket of his coat. "And you'll see just how deranged Prendick was once we get inside."

He was quite right – the sight of the place beyond that heavy door was as chilling as any murder scene. The entrance hall was simple enough – a slate floor, a large table in its centre with a lacklustre vase of dried flowers on it. But there the normality ceased. In a band around the walls someone had written the same phrase over and over again: *Fear the Law.* The letters ranged from the minute, precise hand of an obsessive, to the wild daubs of a man gripped by a terrifying rage.

"I'm pretty sure he wrote them himself," said Mann, "not only because it was a phrase that cropped up frequently in his original statement to the sailors who rescued him, but also because the words are written at the right height, and he had a habit of using a typographical 'a' with the curl at the top rather than the more conventional handwritten style." He opened the folder of notes he had been carrying. "I have a number of address labels from the post office that show him using the same form. Not conclusive perhaps but as close as I need to be satisfied."

"Surely the cleaner…"

"Had never seen the like! I assume the writing was the first symptom of the mania that brought him to kill himself."

"But what brought it on?" I thought back to our previous conversation. "You say he received some post on the Wednesday – what was it?"

He checked his notes again while I walked around the entrance hall, reading the daubs on the wall. "A parcel of aluminium phosphide…"

"Rodenticide," I said. "Any sign of traps around the place?"

"Everywhere. According to Mrs Bradley, he was obsessive about them."

"Terrified of animals," I said. "Given his history, that would make sense."

"Indeed it would." Mann closed his notes and wandered to the window. It was clear this wasn't a thought that had occurred to him. "Maybe he saw something – a rat or mouse perhaps – through the window. An animal could have been his trigger, you think?"

"If it was then it's surprising he survived so long."

Mann turned and raised an eyebrow. Then nodded. "Living out here he must have come across all manner of creatures," he agreed. "If he were that fragile a flock of Old Brandon's sheep would have been enough to have him reaching for the acid cabinet."

"Any other post?"

"A religious pamphlet, a chemistry journal and a copy of *The Times*."

"He was a subscriber?"

"I presume so. To be honest I didn't check. You're wondering whether someone sent it to him specifically?"

I shrugged. "If someone were trying to get a message to him, or intimidate him somehow then that could be a method. Of course, it all rather depends what was in the paper." The obvious thought occurred to me. "Anything about the mutilated bodies found in Rotherhithe?"

"I would have thought so," he said. "What paper isn't filling its column inches with that story? You telling me there might be a link?"

"There might at that," I agreed. "Though I'm probably not allowed to say more." The look on his face was not favourable. "I know," I said, holding my hands up in a placatory fashion, "I have no wish to be secretive, but Holmes and I have been employed in a governmental capacity and I genuinely don't know how much I should say." The minute the words were out of my mouth I found I was regretting them. Mann was clearly a decent fellow and I had no doubt he would be trustworthy. But then that was hardly my decision to make.

"Policemen do not take kindly to being kept in the dark, Dr Watson," he said. "It's inimical to their profession."

"I appreciate that," I said. "And if it were up to me…"

"Aye, well, it seems to me that, as you're a private individual, I shouldn't even be letting you in here." He looked at me pointedly. "But I made an exception."

I sighed. It was extremely tempting simply to unburden myself on the man. But, aside from my gut instinct, what did I really have to go on? I had met him on only two occasions, and on both of those occasions he had seemed a capable officer and a reliable fellow. But that was hardly enough when I had been sworn to secrecy by one of the highest figures in the country.

"I understand how you feel," I said eventually. "And if I have to leave, then so be it. But I really can't say more for now. I have been sworn to secrecy and I cannot break that vow, however much my personal estimation of you insists it would be safe to do so. It is not my secret to keep and therefore the decision as to who knows and who does not is not mine to make."

He nodded and, after a moment, smiled. "Don't twist yourself in knots over it. I suppose I should be glad of the fact that you won't betray a trust so easily, it proves that I was right to share police information with you. Doesn't mean it's not extremely irritating, mind, but let's forget it…"

I was relieved and said so.

"It won't be the first time a simple copper from the countryside has not been privy to the same information as everyone else," he said. "In fact it happens so often you'd think I wouldn't bat an eyelid."

He led me through into the next room, a small library and office that betrayed the state of its owner's mind as clearly as the entrance hall had. Books were cast all over, paper thrown everywhere. It was as if a small stick of dynamite had detonated in there – indeed, some of the pages were burned, which only increased the illusion. Of course the dynamite in this case had been none other than Edward Prendick, a man whose moods had clearly been easily combustible.

"It's hard to tell whether he was trying to destroy something in particular or just on a rampage," said Mann. "The rest of the house is in a similar state."

I stooped down to look at some of the papers; for the most part they were chemistry text books, Prendick's own notes and part of what must have been an obsessive collection of old newspapers and magazines. "He was certainly a hoarder," I said, rummaging through a pile of yellowing newspapers. "There are what must be a year's worth of copies of *The Chronicle* here."

"For a man who disliked society so much," said Mann, "it seems strange he took such an interest in it."

I could see his point, but it seemed more likely to me that Prendick's motivations had been different. I didn't think he was monitoring current affairs out of general interest. Rather he was monitoring the news for mention of something in particular. If he had been as shaken by Moreau's work as had clearly been the case, was it not natural that he might look for evidence of it? Perhaps another scientist might stumble upon the same methods, or the creatures he so feared might make their way off their island and come in search of new pastures. Prendick's fear was all-consuming. If he hadn't been mad when they lifted him off his makeshift raft in the ocean, then he had certainly become so during the years after.

The question remained though: was it suicide or murder? All the evidence pointed to the former but there was still a big part of me that sensed the hand of another – someone who might have driven Prendick to the chemistry supplies and a lunatic urge to destroy himself. I was convinced the answers must lie in the last-known postal delivery.

"I don't suppose you still have the mail he received?" I asked.

Mann nodded. "We haven't the space out here to keep all our evidence ad infinitum, but we haven't cleared anything of Prendick's out yet. Given the court's ruling, you can help yourself to what you like. I'll have no use for it."

CHAPTER TWENTY

We continued our tour around Prendick's cottage, but there was little else I wanted to see. It was a broken and depressing place, somewhere a fractured mind had been left to burn white-hot during its last few hours. The damage was extensive, the explanations few. My hope was that worthwhile answers might be found in the evidence store of the local constabulary, as it was conspicuously lacking here.

We left the cottage and walked back into town. Mann had appeared to dismiss all of his previous irritation over my secrecy. As we walked, he chatted about his time on the force and how long he had lived here, as well as listing a number of the more colourful citizens. He painted a picture of a comfortable, pleasant career, albeit one that he felt was incapable of stretching his abilities. I wondered how long he would manage compromising one part of his life for the satisfaction of another. To hear him talk it was obvious that he wouldn't be able to ignore his need to shine as a detective. His frustration – and the frequent comments about how rural policemen

were perceived – showed how heavily it weighed on him and I had
no doubt that we would see him in the city before long.

Constable Scott greeted us once more as we entered the station,
uttering his words around the thick obstacle of a mouthful of
sandwich.

"Lunch on duty, Scott?" Mann asked, though he appeared not in
the least concerned.

"Constable Wright's off sick, Sir," Scott explained. "So I'm on my
own today. It don't bother me if it don't bother the glorious public."

"I'm sure they'll have seen worse, Constable, carry on."

Scott did so, chasing a pickled egg around his lunch pail with a
gleeful look on his face.

We passed Mann's office and he led me to a door at the very
rear of the station. He drew a large bunch of keys from his pocket,
selected the correct one and let us in. We found ourselves in a small
storeroom lined with row after row of shelving.

"Not exactly the Black Museum," he said. "But it does for us."

He worked his way along the rows, running a finger along the
edge of the shelving as he counted off the case numbers. Finding
the box he wanted, he pulled it free and carried it over to a central
table.

"This is everything we have," he said, unfastening the lid and
beginning to lay the contents out on the table. "The newspaper…"
He handed it to me and I glanced through it. The story about the
Rotherhithe murders was certainly present in the form of a lengthy
report and editorial. Though, as Mann himself had said, that in
itself didn't necessarily mean anything. It had been one of the
biggest stories of recent weeks so any paper of that date would be
likely to cover it.

"The religious pamphlet," Mann announced, handing me a small, cream-coloured booklet. *HE is not dead*, the cover announced –

HE has changed HIS shape. HE has changed HIS body. For a time you will not see HIM. HE is above where he can watch you. You cannot see HIM. But HE can see you.

"The usual intimidating scripture," said Mann. "These people rarely seem to preach the words of a kindly God."

"You recognise the quote?" I asked.

"No," he admitted, "and I usually can." He smiled sheepishly. "My father was a lay preacher and that sort of thing sticks. At one point I could probably quote the whole Bible backwards." He looked at the pamphlet. "It doesn't even read right," he said. "'He has changed his shape'?" That's hardly biblical phrasing. They could have done their reading a little better. No doubt it's from some nutty apocrypha."

He returned his attention to the box. "We don't have the poison," he said. "Prendick had already put a good deal of it to use. Proof of his obsession, he unpacked that first! But we do have a selection of his papers. This –" he lifted out a wrapped bundle of pages that put me in mind of nothing less than the manuscript of a novel "– deals specifically with his time at sea. It makes for fascinating reading, though I can't say I believed a word of it. I think I'd have put it down as a novel, one of those scientific romances, were it not for the fact that I could see the state of the author's mind for myself."

"Might I borrow some of these items?" I asked. "I know it's a great deal to ask…"

"As far as the law is concerned the case is closed. Take what you like, if his family come chasing any of it then I'll be in touch."

"Are there any family, then?" I had assumed Prendick had been quite alone in the world.

"Aye, though they were quick enough to distance themselves from him when he started going on about cat people. The only one I've met is a nephew, Charles, he was sniffing around at the inquest. Trying to decide if there was any money to be had, if you ask me. I didn't rank him as a suspect."

I bundled Prendick's notes along with those of Mitchell's, added the newspaper and – on an impulse – the religious pamphlet.

"I'll make a note of it," said Mann, "though it would have only ended up gathering dust until we need to clear out to make more space."

He admitted that he had a great deal of real casework to be getting on with, so I left Mann to it and made my way back to the Dog and Sheep to pass the time before the next train back to London.

I sat in a corner booth and began to read Mitchell's notes on his time working with Moreau. It made for disturbing reading – a seemingly endless list of abuses towards the animal test subjects with little or no potential benefit that I could see. I washed the sour taste away with a pint of the excellent local beer and transferred my attention to Prendick's writing.

Mann was right in that it read like a novel, and I found myself considerably engrossed in its narrative. Prendick wrote with a cold, slightly neurotic style but that was no great surprise given what I knew of the man's personality. The notes told of his time on the ill-fated lifeboat from the *Lady Vain* followed by his rescue at the hands of Montgomery, who had been aboard a ship transporting provisions to the island where he lived and worked with Moreau. Put ashore by the boat's crew – the surly captain unwilling to take

Prendick any further after a disagreement with Montgomery – Prendick was trapped with the two scientists and their motley crew of natives. From there the narrative grew stranger still but, noticing that I would only narrowly avoid missing my train, I curtailed my reading and made a run for the station.

The journey back to London saw me return to the South Pacific, following Prendick's saga as first he realised the identity of the man he had been stranded with, then encountered the products of that man's work – the strange creatures that seemed to thrive in the central jungle of that small island. I fully understood why Mann had dismissed it as the notions of a lunatic, but I did not have that comfortable luxury. I knew from what Mycroft had told us that a great deal of Prendick's notes were true. I was feeling ill at ease by the time I arrived at Liverpool Street – these were murky waters indeed.

Hopeful that Holmes would be at Baker Street, I was impatient to tell him of my day thus far and so engaged a cab at the station.

On arriving home, I paid the driver and let myself in. A loud crashing of furniture from upstairs told me that my colleague was indeed home. Such a noise didn't disturb me in the least. Regular readers will be aware of the fact that Holmes was a law unto himself, and a frequently destructive one. I once had to console Mrs Hudson for an entire evening after he had destroyed one of her sofas with a wrecking hammer, wishing to test "the tensile resistance of mahogany". Naturally he paid for such cruelties towards the furnishings, but it didn't stop our landlady suffering frequent bouts of nerves.

"What are you doing this time, Holmes?" I asked as I entered. "If Mrs Hudson's at home you'd better prepare yourself for a firm admonishing."

"That's already in hand, Watson," my friend replied in a somewhat pinched voice.

The voice was pinched because of the large, leather mitten that held him by the throat. The mitten belonging to Kane, the deformed gang leader we had thought ourselves fortunate enough to have left behind in the tunnels beneath Rotherhithe.

"What perfect timing, Watson," said Holmes. "Might you be good enough to come to my assistance?"

Since when did he have to ask? I dropped the papers I was carrying and marched over to wrestle Kane – a big man he may have been but I had no doubt the two of us would be a match for him. But he knocked me backwards as soon as I was in reach of those thick arms, sending me tumbling over a footstool to sprawl on my back on the hearth-rug.

"If you could perhaps try a little harder than that?" Holmes managed to ask, desperately trying to pull the clamped mitten from his throat before it crushed the life out of him.

I grasped the poker and set at the man's shoulders. I would like to say that, as a medical man, I was only too aware of the safe areas to hit Kane but it would be a lie. At that point I cared little for the gang leader's longevity, I simply wished to see him fall and my friend removed from his potentially lethal grip. Kane roared and the noise was deafening. He dropped Holmes and turned to face me. I was pleased I had succeeded in one of my aims, though concerned that I would soon be in just as dire a situation as Holmes had been.

Holmes fell to the floor, rubbing at his throat.

"If you could return the favour?" I asked.

"Certainly," he replied and made a dash for his bedroom.

Perplexed – and not a little irritated – I did my best to keep

Kane at bay by swinging the poker forward and back in a large arc. He batted at it with those large hands of his and kept coming. I imagined that deformed face beneath the veil of netting he wore – that terrible, open wound of a mouth, gnashing and drooling as he backed me into the corner.

"Holmes!" I shouted. "My revolver's in my undergarment drawer!"

"Of course it is," he replied, having returned to the room, "but I have something altogether more effective."

I saw he had the small pipe he had used before, the device he had refused to explain, in his petulant mood. He raised it to his lips and blew.

If it were – as I had originally suspected – some form of blowpipe, there was no sign of a dart. Nonetheless, Kane stopped dead in his tracks. With an animal howl he raised his hands to his head and then toppled backwards, crashing to the floor like a felled tree.

"What the devil is that?" I asked.

Holmes held it up with a chuckle. "I present the Perry Canine Remonstration Pod, purloined off the good professor during our meeting at the museum."

"The what?" I was baffled at my friend's explanation, baffled all the more when he reached forward and yanked the net-lined hat Kane had been wearing. Underneath was the head of a gigantic hound!

PART THREE

THE TERRIBLE FATHER

CHAPTER TWENTY-ONE

"You knew?" I asked Holmes. "Even when we were in the sewers you knew that Kane was one of these monstrous hybrids?"

"I guessed as much from his mannerisms," he agreed. "The way he moved, the way he sniffed the air, his preternaturally sensitive hearing... On the subject of which, should we ever again find ourselves faced with an opponent able to hear a pin drop at a thousand yards kindly don't call me by name, I may as well have left the brute a business card."

I hadn't been aware of having done so but there was little point in arguing. I apologised and squatted down to give Kane a closer examination. The head was exactly like that of a dog, a bull mastiff, given its size and crumpled features. The hair was short and black with a dusting of white on its muzzle.

"What luck you had that whistle," I said. "How long do you think it will last?"

"Oh, next to no time at all I imagine," he said, dashing off to fetch a heavy pair of derbies he kept on top of the bookcase. "And it wasn't luck," he shouted, climbing his way past his collection of foreign dictionaries. "We were promised monstrous animal hybrids and one of the professors has a device for disabling dogs. I would have been stupid not to take it."

"And if Kane had been half cat?" I asked as he dropped back down and began to fix the handcuffs around the creature's wrists.

"Well," he said, getting to his feet, "then I would have dangled some thread in front of it."

I had loosened its collar, eager to judge the physiognomy beneath its heavy coat. At the base of its furry throat there was a heavy knot of scar tissue betraying where a large incision had been made. Was it simply a dog's head attached to a human body? Surely not, for now I realised the point of its heavy leather mittens. Removing one I was presented with the large black hand of an ape. Everything about Kane was built for strength and aggression it seemed.

The creature began to move, the eyelids flickering and opening slowly. I stood up and took a couple of steps back. Curiosity was one thing, but I didn't want its teeth at our throats over my unanswered questions. There would be time enough for further examination once it was secure in police custody.

"Shall I send Billy to fetch the police?" I asked, referring to Holmes' page boy. "Surely the sooner the brute is locked up the better?"

"Oh, I don't know," said Holmes, dropping into his armchair and lighting his pipe, "I rather thought it might be to all our advantages were we to pool our resources." He looked pointedly at the creature between us, now clearly conscious and eyeing us both cautiously. "Wouldn't you say, Kane?"

The voice when it came had an animal growl that, now I knew

its biological background, was not in the least surprising. What I had taken before as a gruff tone was nothing less than the sound of human speech being forced through a dog's throat.

"What advantage would there be for me?" it asked.

"Oh come now!" said Holmes. "What interest do I have in your petty underground activities? I'm dealing with a far bigger picture than street crime, however well-organised, however brutal. I want your creator, I want the man who made you who you are. Give me him and you can go free for all I care."

"Holmes!" I exclaimed. This was hardly the first time my colleague had taken the law into his own hands, but there was a world of difference between defending those who had committed dark acts for the best of reasons and protecting a violent street criminal simply because his information might be useful. No doubt the police may have had cause to strike such bargains in the course of their investigations – I am not naive as to the methods they sometimes have to employ in order to achieve the greater good – but I was distinctly uncomfortable at being complicit in such an arrangement.

"We must look to the case as a whole, Watson. There is a great deal more at stake here than a little pickpocketing and smuggling."

"How right you are," Kane said. "If my father has anything to say about matters, then all of England will soon be shaken by the throat."

"Father?" Holmes said. "You think of him as that?"

"In the sense that he created me, not with any emotional feeling. I'll happily tell you all you want to know about him."

Holmes brought his knees up to his chin and sucked hard on his pipe. "Then kindly do so," he said, making a theatrical, beckoning gesture with his hands. "Tell me all you know."

CHAPTER TWENTY-TWO

"I call him my father but in that he was one of many. That is why he grew to hate me. Fathers, like gods, are quick to grow angry at others who claim their title. The special creatures he has sired, the pure-bloods, who find their life through scalpel and needle, are perfect in his eyes. He loves them dearly. But those like me, his mongrels, built from a butcher's shop of ingredients, to him we are nothing, we are empty and worthless creatures.

"But I am far from empty, I am filled with lives lived. I remember the warmth of the litter and the taste of sweet milk. I remember the feel of thick grass parting before me as I run, the sound of a rabbit's heartbeat in my ears and the taste of its fear once it's in my mouth. I remember the sun on my back and salt wind in my face – a face that now rots, torn away and left to decay; the feel of tarred rope in my hands and the solid decking shifting beneath my feet as the waves throw me towards the sky. I remember the pull of rope around my throat and the glint of a belt buckle in the gaslight; the feel of leather cracking against my back.

"I remember that last best of all and I tell you, Gentlemen, no man will strike me again without knowing consequences, not now I have the strength to strike back.

"How I fell into the hands of that final, terrible father of mine is simple enough. Some of me was sold to him by the man with the eager belt and strong swinging arm. The rest was acquired by criminal means. I have a memory of the taste of beer in my mouth, shore leave and the need to spend the few pennies in your pocket. I was abroad in the backstreets, unsteady due to drink and hopeful of finding someone to keep me warm for a few hours. Then there was the most terrible pain on the back of my head and the next thing I know, I'm waking up on a bed of straw, the stink of animal scat and rotten food in my nostrils. If I had owned the nose you see now, this fine organ that would know what your landlady was cooking for supper as soon as twitch, then I think that smell would have driven me mad. But maybe I'm wrong, maybe what the sailor found distasteful would have been like fresh fruit to me now – so many things have changed, my tastes more than anything else.

"As he screamed and shouted, yanking at the irons that had been placed around his hands and legs – irons like these, Gentlemen, and do not think that I will tolerate them long, for I won't – the hound that had cowered in fear at the sound of its master's tread cowered still, its simple mind not knowing what lay ahead. But then, how could it have predicted it? No beast, walking on two legs or four, could have had the first idea what was in store.

"The future was darkness. The prick of a needle, like an insect bite, that hid the cut of a scalpel. There were many times when I experienced consciousness, for the process was not one operation but a whole string of them. I awoke with shifting agonies from the many incisions all over my body. The terror felt when the mind of that old sailor, a man who remembered everything from the burn of rope to a woman's cheeks gracing his palms, looked at the abomination now attached to his wrists – terrible, ugly, brutal things! Hands made for violence and harm. Hands made to beat and punch, something he had more than enough anger for.

"Then, a few hours later, awake again and the knowledge that he has acquired a tail, an angry, thrashing thing that beats at the back of his legs like a whip, spurring him on like a slave. Oh that makes him angry, that makes him *boil*! But still there is no freedom and soon the darkness descends again and the knives part flesh and sew meat.

"I understand the problems of such operations, the impossibility of making one creature's muscles tug at another's limbs, and I cannot begin to explain how he makes it work. I know that he was not always successful. There are many chambers that run alongside his workroom filled with his failures. Creatures that shout, or mew, or bark, or chirp like birds as they hurl their useless flesh against the walls, flesh that bubbles and rejects itself, falling off in lumps or swelling up in angry, purple balloons. Some of these creatures are useful deterrents, terrifying monstrosities that act as guards and weapons, happy to vent their terror and fury on whatever or whoever he wishes them to attack. Others are little more than walking supply cupboards, living cultures that he raids for parts and organs whenever he has need. You do not know real misery, Gentlemen, until you have lain on cold stone and listened to the sound of abomination praying for death! Abomination that bears more than a passing resemblance to your own reflection in the glass.

"That final series of operations: where my throat bristled and burned with nerve-endings yanked together like a boatman's twine; my eyes raged in their sockets at the bright lights, my mouth screaming wider than the height of my own head. It took him a week to change that head, a connection at a time, a cut here and a cut there.

"And then there was the work he undertook within my skull, replacing one brain with parts of another. I have lost a few handfuls of this tissue along the way, Gentlemen. I heard them fall onto the cool stone behind me while he cut and tore. But don't think it's made me a fool, for I manage only too well with what I have. It hurts, by God it does. My head feels like its splitting most of the time. But, after a while, pain becomes just another thing you accept. You know how a stench in a room can vanish after you've been in it a while? The familiarity makes the nose ignore it. Pain is like that once you've suffered it for long enough. I think his work has helped there too. I am not as sensitive as I once was. Sometimes when I pick up an object, I crush it quite by accident, it's so difficult to feel.

"Finally, it was done and I have the face you see now – a face that roars, a mouth with teeth that can tear through flesh like a fistful of knives. Not that I often have cause to use them, not on living flesh at least. I may be a monster in the eyes of most, but I try to be a civilised one. Oh yes, you doubt that, given my profession. Well, perhaps I am not the perfect citizen but I don't hurt for the sake of it, however tempting it might be. And it is tempting, Gentlemen, you have no idea how strong the urge rises within me when I look upon your fragile, pink faces. Sometimes I think there's nothing that would feel better than taking them between my jaws and snapping these teeth of mine shut. I always knew anger, all of me – the sailor and the hound. But now we are combined. Lord! I sometimes wonder that there can be so much rage in any one creature.

"But I control it. Yes, because I will not be the worthless creature my father considers me. I will be better than they could ever have dreamt. I will be a thing of wonder, not an atrocity; a thing that makes a man's lip curl in disgust.

"For that's the first thing these new eyes saw, looking up into the face of the man that stitched them into place – disgust. You might think that a man would take some pride in his work, would create a thing he wanted to see. Apparently not. When my father looked down on this, this… *body*, this… *creature* that he had spent so many weeks – so many hours of work, so much *effort* – creating, his only response was repulsion and disappointment. I ask you, what is the point of that? What did he think he was building with his offal-stained fingers?

"No matter. I was a thing to be ignored. He gave me lowly tasks, manual jobs that suited my strong arms. Outside of those tasks I was ignored so I made the most of the fact. I hunted in the tunnels, learning the geography of the under-city, where I still make my home. Why would I rise to the city above? I belong down there, flushed away with the rest of the waste, hidden in the dark, forgotten.

"I worked my way through father's library, reading – though not always understanding – his books and notes. I tried to better myself, to be more than he believed me to be. Perhaps I sought approval. Why lie? I *know* I sought it. But there was no approval to be found. He was too all-consumed with the children he made after me, refining his science, learning new techniques and experimenting with new ideas. I was no more interesting than a sketch on a piece of scrap paper, rolled into a ball and tossed to one side.

"Is it any wonder I wished for freedom?

"I began to appreciate the fact that I was almost invisible within the confines of those tunnels and chambers. I watched father work, noting his methods, trying to understand his plans. That understanding, with every stab of pain it brought upon this ruin of a brain I have, was knowledge hard-earned but I think I have his measure now. In fact I know I do. Because there's one thing that will always retain its value, Gentlemen – knowledge, and with it I am wealthy indeed.

"Once I felt I had understood all I could, I decided the time had come to leave my father's company. My time there would always have been short, he was never a man satisfied with the quantity or quality of materials, and sooner or later I would represent a greater value to him as organs and tissue as I did as – yes, the joke is clear – as his dogsbody. I would sit and feed the other creatures left to rot in their cells, watching as some of them diminished, driven mad by pain or infection, crippled further and further by scalpel or saw, and I resolved never to join them. Whatever the shortcomings of this grotesque form it – and the life within it – is all I have and I intend to keep hold of it for as long as possible.

"Father was not permanently in residence so leaving was never going to be difficult. He could sometimes be absent for days at a time. I couldn't say whether he was gathering fresh subjects or simply going about a life outside that he kept hidden away beneath the streets. To be frank I didn't care. I simply waited for his next absence and took my opportunity. Only too aware that my appearance would be a handicap, I adopted a rough version of the costume you see before you and made my way to the surface. Though I had never left father's lair, the route was extremely simple; I had cause to be thankful of this sensitive nose of mine as it sniffed out his trail all the way to the surface.

"And what a world that now seemed to me! The noises were more grating, the smells sharper. It was a world that hurt just to be in it, a place that beat at the senses. I stumbled upon a small man selling roasted chestnuts and was nearly paralysed by the experience. As if his shouting were not enough, there was the roar of his fire, the crackle of the nutshells, the hiss and pop of coals fracturing, the chink of metal expanding in the heat. Then the smell, the smoke, the browning meat of the nuts, the sweat of the man – his stench alone was like a factory floor.

"It felt like being attacked. It was all I could do not to tear out his throat in response. My temper is not good, Gentlemen, as you will have no doubt remarked. Perhaps you begin to understand why?

"It was soon clear to me that I could not tolerate a normal life above ground. A piece of the underground was the place for me. I am a creature that suits shadow, am I not?

"But what could I do? How should I provide for myself?

"Oh I dare say you do not approve of my solution to that problem, but I have finished seeking approval from you or anyone else. Criminality is something I am suited to. I have the anger and strength for it. And yes, I have a lack of consideration towards 'my fellow man'. For, let us be honest, there is no such thing anymore is there, Gentlemen? I am a species all of its own.

"Nonetheless, my business matters are sure to be beneath your concern, Mr Holmes. What do you care if the inventory of a ship becomes light once in a while? Is it any business of yours if the walking wounded of our society take to the opium pipe? Why should Sherlock Holmes, London's greatest consulting detective, trouble himself if a little counterfeit money works its way into the system? I have very little blood on my hands, Gentlemen, and the few stains there are came from men who work the same business as I. It is not something that troubles me.

"And it must not trouble you if you wish my assistance in this matter, and you do, believe me, for who else do you know that can lead you straight to the door of the man you seek? Who else knows the details of what he is planning? Who else can salvage this mess before the country is brought to its knees?

"Gentlemen, I rather think you and I are going into business!"

CHAPTER TWENTY-THREE

The brute leaned forward, those monstrous hands extended as he jangled the handcuffs that hung from them. His tale was done, his point made.

Holmes merely watched for a moment and then laughed.

"You are a confident fellow, Kane," he said, "and I'll warrant that your extraordinary life so far would have broken a lesser spirit. Still, I will tell you this: you ask what concern it is of mine that you pursue your criminal career. You talk of London's greatest consulting detective?" The apparent lightness of tone faded from Holmes' voice to be replaced by a steel that was as sharp and potent as a sabre-blade. "I am the foremost consulting detective in the *country*, Kane, no doubt the world, and your criminal activities are every bit my concern. Furthermore, the moment I wish them to end I could ensure it happened as quickly as that." He snapped his fingers for emphasis. "You bet with an empty hand," he continued, "and your pitiful attempts to intimidate me impress me not one jot.

If you know a scintilla of useful information about your creator then you have yet to prove as much, certainly you will have to work hard to convince me that what you know is worth my turning a blind eye to so much as a day's worth of your petty little enterprises." He sat back in his chair and took a long puff on his pipe. "You will have to work much harder than this to preserve your scarred neck," he said, exhaling a cloud of smoke towards the sensitive nose of our prisoner. "We have you captured and entirely at our mercy. If you wish to survive the encounter I suggest you begin to talk of something more useful than your own pathetic history."

Kane roared and jumped to his feet, the chair he was sat on tumbling behind him. He pulled at his handcuffs but they held firm, not that his greatest strength lay at the end of his wrists. He snarled and those teeth of his dripped with malice.

There was a soft click as Holmes cocked the revolver he had just removed from his dressing gown pocket. With a raised eyebrow he uttered one world only, a word designed to enrage our captive even further: "Sit!"

Kane had little choice but to do so, though he howled at the indignity of it.

"That's better," Holmes replied. "As powerful as you no doubt are, a bullet through the skull would bring you to heel."

I began to realise quite how much he was enjoying this. I hoped it didn't see him get his throat torn out.

Kane growled and then began to speak further:

"I have said that I have not sought the death of others and that the blood on my hands is meagre." He looked at Holmes, cocking his head on one side in that peculiar way that dogs have when they are particularly drawn by something. "That may soon change.

I have no doubt that to have your head in my jaws would be a pleasurable thing indeed."

"Well, metaphorically at least, I certainly have yours in mine," said Holmes, "so let us get to business before either of us sees fit to bite."

"Father has not just been working as a surgeon," Kane continued. "He has been hard at work in the field of chemistry too. He has been attempting to create a serum that can change the flesh without a need for the scalpel."

"Change the flesh how?" I asked, though I could imagine the answer after what Mycroft had told us.

"He wishes to accelerate the process of evolution. The example he gave – and I am only too aware of how fanciful it sounds – was of a man falling from a great height. What use is evolution then? If it could respond immediately to the body's surroundings then it could be the very thing that saves his life! He could sprout wings!"

I laughed, the idea certainly did sound fanciful. The subtle changes Mycroft had suggested, such as an ability to last longer than natural without water, or an increased tolerance to the cold, had sounded absurd enough. But this – the spontaneous growth of new appendages? What next, would a man on a windy day suddenly develop iron feet? Or a drowning man, gills?

"Yes," said Kane, "that was my response too. Then I looked in a mirror and, try as I might, I could no longer find the same confidence in my opinions."

Holmes thought about this for a moment then spoke: "The fact that he is experimenting in this field means nothing," he said. "We knew as much already, the question is rather: is he making any progress?" He looked intently at Kane, as if trying to determine whether he could trust him. How he could hope to tell was utterly beyond me – what could one look to in that animal's face to serve as a sign of veracity?

"I think you will soon know the answer to that," Kane said. "It will not be long before my father acts, but can you afford to wait until then?"

"The bodies," said Holmes. "Can I presume they were the victims of these creatures you described? The monstrous hybrids he keeps as guard dogs to his lair?"

Kane appeared to shrug, and somehow this small, human gesture seemed the most absurd thing he had done thus far, to see something so recognisable come from something so inhuman. "Every now and then people would wander into his lair, and he would have me dispose of the bodies elsewhere. Now that I am not there to do his dirty work no doubt they simply wash up where they are wont to."

Holmes sat in silence for another couple of moments then got to his feet. He handed the gun to me and walked over to Kane.

"Needless to say, you should shoot our visitor the moment he looks like wishing to do either of us damage," he said. "I will ensure that you have a clear shot."

I was distinctly unhappy about the idea of letting Kane go free but I was also sufficiently intimidated by him that I decided it was better to show a united front and keep my concerns to myself. Holmes would do whatever he wished and all that would be achieved by us arguing over it would be a distraction that the vicious creature may take advantage of.

Holmes unfastened the handcuffs and stood well back. He gestured to the door.

"Go," he said, "but know that our arrangement is not carved in stone. I have preparations to make before I follow you to the lair of your creator. If you prove to be a valuable guide then it will go some way towards the freedom I allow you to operate under in Rotherhithe." He pointed at Kane. "But know this – don't think you are immune from my attentions. If I consider that you step outside the incestuous world of gang violence and become a threat to the innocent then I will find you and put an end to you. Is that understood?"

Kane inclined his head and I tried to decide if his exposed teeth represented a threat or a sign of humour. Perhaps it was both. "It is understood that you will try," he said. "How long do you need to prepare?"

"Return here this evening at nine o'clock, I will be accompanied by a small party."

"Police?" Kane asked. An unmistakable growl to his words.

"No," Holmes replied, "private citizens, but ones whom you can rely upon to offer a degree of strength against the creatures we might find down there."

Kane nodded and once again that half-smile, half-snarl was visible on his face. "They'll need it," he said, and bounded down the stairs and out of our rooms.

CHAPTER TWENTY-FOUR

Once Kane had left, Holmes visibly relaxed and settled back into his armchair. He reclaimed his pipe and brought it back to life with a match. "An unnerving character, Watson," he said. "Only a fool argues with the clear evidence of his own eyes. Still, to be face to face with such a beast. To converse with it…"

"I've never seen anything like it," I admitted.

"It is a nightmare of flesh," he concurred. "The sort of vision one might suffer after indulging in that opium pipe he made such light business of."

"He made light business of a great deal of criminal behaviour," I said. "It's a wonder you let him leave."

He shrugged. "What choice did I have? I no more trust him than I like him but the stakes are high and we must take every advantage offered. I strongly suspect that the minute we descend into that damp 'under-city' our lives will be fragile things indeed, but we must try. Who knows what that creature's creator has planned? Are we dealing with a lunatic with ideas beyond his ability or, much worse, are we dealing with a man who can achieve the monstrous acts he claims he is capable of?"

"A serum that forces the human body to adapt? I cannot credit it."

"In truth, nor can I but the risk of the consequences if we are both wrong is too great to bear."

He settled to think for a moment, no doubt imagining the possible effects of such a chemical. What chaos it could wreak if let loose into the world!

I settled into the chair opposite him and reached for my own cigarettes. What manner of creature would Holmes become if exposed to such a concoction – a swollen brain hovering over a pair of massive, tobacco-hardened lungs? The thought of such a beast, despite the serious context, could not help but make me smile.

"And what of you?" he said, intruding into my thoughts. "A massive heart and stomach perhaps?"

"Steady on, Holmes," I replied, "there's no need to be offensive." I didn't acknowledge that he had guessed what I had been thinking. I wouldn't give him the satisfaction. It was a damnable trick and not the first time he'd played it.

Which reminded me of how I had spent the majority of my day. "You may be able to read my more obvious thoughts, Holmes," I said. "But even you will not be able to plumb the depths, I have a great deal to tell you!"

"Your investigations went well did they?" he replied.

I concede that for a moment I was more than a little put out. "My investigations?"

"Well obviously you've been looking into the matter, you've been out all day and were no doubt positively itching to prove your deductive capabilities."

"Only because you have been so damnably smug of late!"

He raised an eyebrow. "Only of late?" He offered a smile. "You know my moods, Watson my friend, better than any other. I apologise for my recent behaviour. I would say that it won't happen again but we both know that's a promise I'll struggle to keep."

In a way Holmes was even more irritating when he capitulated; you wanted to rage at the man and all he could do was nod and admit he was annoying. If there was a better way of taking the wind from a man's sails I didn't know of it.

"You are quite the most irritating man I know."

"I excel in all things then," he replied and chuckled. "But come! Tell me of your adventures."

Seeing little point in arguing further, I did as he asked. I picked up the folder containing Prendick's account and the papers I had been given by Mitchell.

"Watson," Holmes announced once I had finished, "if I ever suggest you are anything less than a marvel remind me of today, you have done extremely well."

Despite my previous irritation I couldn't help but be pleased. "I must admit that I was concerned that I was hardly farther forward than when I began," I admitted. "The mystery seems thicker rather than clearer."

"These matters are murky indeed," he admitted, "but you have certainly gathered data that solves some of the loose ends. In fact you have given me most of what I need to complete my own deductions."

"Complete them?"

"Indeed. Prendick's death seemed deeply unsatisfactory to me and that is at last brought into clarity."

"Unsatisfactory?" That seemed hardly a humane word to use in the context.

He tutted at my faint disapproval. "You know full well what I mean," he said. "Viewed from a purely logical perspective – as I always must, these matters will not solve themselves by my emoting all over them – it presented a number of complications. Why was acid used? It immediately made one suspect that the body was not that of Prendick but rather someone else entirely, the acid an attempt to disfigure the corpse so extensively it would be impossible to tell."

I admitted that the thought had occurred to me.

"Of course it had, Mycroft too I have no doubt. But it would seem from what Inspector Mann tells us that the face was perfectly clear. So why such a painful method?"

"I had wondered whether there was a degree of self-hatred involved," I said. "He chose a painful method because he believed he deserved to suffer."

Holmes shook his head. "Someone who wishes to suffer does not end their life." He suddenly clapped his hands. "Of course! It was a preventative measure! He wanted to destroy his organs so that they would be of no further use. He was terrified of some part of him ending up inside another creature."

"It's a possibility," I agreed.

"A certainty, he must have had a good reason to endure such suffering and it's the only one that fits."

I began to leaf through his account of matters on the island. "This is quite the most bizarre thing you'll ever read," I said.

"No," said Holmes, fetching his hat and coat, "for one day you'll write its sequel! Gather yourself, Watson, we should begin preparations for this evening."

I folded Prendick's account into my pocket and within moments we were in a cab and on our way to a hotel on The Strand.

CHAPTER TWENTY-FIVE

"We need to enlist the rifle of Mr Carruthers," Holmes explained. "It would be foolishness indeed to take on such ferocious beasts without it. While we travel let me tell you how I've occupied my own time, for you can rest assured neither of us have been idle.

"I decided to investigate the two animal dealers Johnson mentioned. Perhaps a trail could be established, leading from the ledger book of one to the illicit laboratory of the other. It was a worthwhile thread to follow.

"Of the two businesses, that of the Welshman, Thomas, seemed the most likely. Johnson had already established that the majority of his trade was to the scientific community. The business is run from a small shop on the Commercial Road. It presents itself as a most innocent affair, a general store like any other."

Holmes gestured offhandedly out of the cab window to illustrate his point.

"A small bell above the door alerted Thomas that he had a

visitor," he continued, "and he emerged from a back room while I was perusing his stock."

Holmes smiled, clearly working his mental way along the memory of the man's shelves.

"He seemed to carry a little of everything as the most successful of those shops inevitably do – from basic ironmongery to reams of cloth; tinned groceries to children's toys. And if you couldn't see it, instructed several hand-printed signs dotted around the place, all you had to do was ask and the management would track it down for you."

"A bold claim!" I said.

"Indeed," Holmes agreed, "though I had little doubt it was true, indeed Thomas repeated it as he emerged through a pair of bead curtains and onto the shop floor.

"'Good morning, Sir,' he said. 'Whatever it is that you're hunting for, merely give the word and I shall find it.'

"I had been browsing through the children's toys at the time, a wooden ark complete with its biblical cargo. I placed a small carved lion on the palm of my hand and showed it to him. 'Might you have any bigger specimens?' I asked."

"Subtle," I laughed.

"We haven't time to waste on pussyfooting around," Holmes replied, "brazen enquiries were the way forward. Thomas was only too happy to match my candour.

"'How big did you have in mind?' he said.

"'I had heard you might be able to provide a full-size example,' I told him, gathering more of the carved animals and holding them out. 'In fact I was led to believe you could provide full-size examples of pretty much any animal I chose to name.'

"He smiled, not willing to admit to anything until he had some assurances. 'As the signs say, Sir, I pride myself on being able to find anything my customers wish to buy. These are difficult times for small businesses and many have chosen to specialise in order to survive in today's modern financial world. I have taken the opposite route. If you want it, I can get it.'

"'Regardless of the law?' I asked.

"He shrugged at that and made a show of disapproval. 'Naturally, Sir,' he said, 'I make it a rule never to come to the attention of the police force. I am merely a businessman doing his best to earn a living.' A nebulous answer!"

"And one designed to reassure the law-breaking customer," I noted.

"Most certainly," he agreed. "I was being invited to commit myself! So I decided to press the point. 'If I, as a gentleman of science, wished to procure experimental stock – live specimens – then you would be able to help me?'

"'Nothing illegal in that,' he said. 'I do a great deal of work with gentlemen of learning such as yourself. It's a noble business, expanding one's knowledge.'

"'Indeed,' I said – in full agreement with that sentiment at least – 'but sometimes one might want to circumnavigate some of the legal procedures, the paperwork in particular. I have no great desire for my rivals to know what sort of experiments I am conducting. In fact I would prefer for nobody to know the details.' Here I decided to leave no room for misunderstanding. "Besides the kind gentleman that might procure such specimens for me in the first place of course.'

"'Naturally,' he replied, 'that could hardly be avoided.' He laughed a little and then decided to try and gain one more piece of security as to my credentials. 'Who was it that suggested I might be able to offer such a service?' he asked. I gave him the name of Moreau and that was enough, Mr Thomas was more than happy to help me and, in so doing, he proved himself the man we were after."

"Amazing that the man's name might be deemed any sign of security," I said.

Holmes nodded. "But you must remember we are dealing with a community that would either endorse Moreau's work or, in Thomas's case, simply not care. These are unpleasant waters." He sighed. "And I'm afraid they remain hard to navigate. The animals are shipped – to Rotherhithe, naturally – and the exchange made at the docks. Thomas retains no paperwork, nor does he have any knowledge of where the animals will end up. It's a blind sale and therefore no use to us in tracking the purchaser down. Nonetheless the encounter answered a number of questions, most particularly with regards his acknowledging the name of Moreau."

"So you believe it's the doctor himself?" I asked. "I haven't got to the section of Prendick's report where he claims to see the man die but I suppose it would only be as accurate as its narrator." I pulled the document free of my pocket and scanned the pages.

"There is a great deal of obfuscation in this case, Watson," he replied. "As always, there is as much to be interpreted from the contradictions and lies as there is from the facts."

It irritated me to admit that I didn't follow.

"People give themselves away as much when they lie as when they tell the truth," Holmes said, "you just have to discern the difference between the two and the reasons behind them.

"For example, Kane said earlier that the bodies found in

Rotherhithe were likely those of people who had simply wandered into his creator's lair. He claimed that he used to dispose of such accidents when he lived there. But now that he was gone, they were left to wash up wherever the tide took them."

"It's a strong tide that washes body parts into a pub."

"Indeed. Not to mention the fact that the second body had been beaten and manacled before being killed, so hardly someone who had simply wandered in and come to an unlucky end."

"Kane may not know that, though."

"Kane's not stupid. He is also clearly obsessed about his creator. To dismiss those bodies as washed-up accidents is not logical. So why did he say it?"

"I don't know, why?"

"My point precisely. Aha! We're here!"

And with that he leapt out of the cab and up the steps of Carruthers' hotel.

CHAPTER TWENTY-SIX

By the time I had paid the driver and caught up with Holmes, he was halfway up the stairs, running towards Carruthers' room.

"Would it not be easier just to meet him in the foyer?" I wondered aloud while catching my breath somewhere on the fifth floor.

"Come on, Watson!" Holmes called. "We haven't time for you to dawdle!"

I made my increasingly breathless way along the corridor of the eighth floor, Holmes a short way ahead, knocking on Carruthers' door.

"Gentlemen!" the explorer shouted on opening the door to greet us, seemingly unconcerned at the fact that he was wearing nothing but a hat and nightshirt. "How splendid to see you! Shall I order breakfast?"

We were forced to explain that it was four o'clock in the afternoon and that perhaps we would be better off taking tea.

"Ah…" He glanced at himself in the mirror and came to realise that perhaps all was not quite how it should be. "I'm afraid I've been scouring the city at night and have quite lost track of my own place in the scheme of things. Perhaps you should order for us and I shall join you in a few moments?"

We agreed that would be for the best and the pair of us made our way back downstairs.

CHAPTER TWENTY-SEVEN

It was no more than ten minutes before we were reacquainted, Carruthers having found a slightly crumpled suit to preserve his modesty before the waiting staff.

"That's better!" he announced, once able to graze on a plate of bread and butter and eye the cake-stand appreciatively. "One forgets to indulge in the niceties."

"Food is a nicety?" I asked with a smile.

"Food that comes on a plate at least," he replied.

"We may well have found you your prey," said Holmes. "Which will save another night of aimless tracking."

"Thank the Lord for that," said Carruthers. "There is nowhere quite so impossible to pin a trail as the city. It has been driving me positively wild."

"I suppose I have grown used to it," said Holmes, "as it has become such a familiar hunting ground to me over the years. Still, even when I think I know every inch of it I stumble upon somewhere new."

"I'm afraid I'm used to areas further afield," Carruthers admitted. "I've spent very little time in the capital. I'm an explorer really, never happier than when I'm far from the place I, somewhat inaccurately, refer to as home."

"Have you always sought game?" I asked.

"Far from it, in fact I'd never claim to be a hunter at all, though certainly I've had occasion to adopt the role. I travel a great deal, as I have mentioned, and tend to find myself drawn to the more dangerous areas of our globe. I have often lent my services to Mycroft's gathering of intelligence. When it came to finding a man who has pitted himself against nature at its most violent and unpredictable, I imagine Mycroft's list was small." He leaned forward in his chair and grinned. "And I dare say most of 'em were far from the capital!"

"It can't have been easy for my brother to find someone whose discretion could be assured," said Holmes.

"Indeed," Carruthers agreed, "the thing with big game hunters is they cannot help but brag, it's part of the sport. How my ears have grown limp listening to interminable tales of unfortunate tigers!"

"Certainly whatever creatures we find are not for show," I said. "These heads are never destined for the games-room wall."

"A fine thing too," said Carruthers. "I've always been more fond of seeing breathing animals than dead ones but, if it's a case of preserving the lives of innocents, then I shall take my shot when I have it."

He leaned back in his chair, finally satiated by the considerable tea platter.

"A number of years ago I was forced to make a similar decision on behalf of a village in the Himalayas. They were besieged by a

wolf pack, regularly losing their children, the animals creeping
into their huts at night and stealing them from their cots.

"The villagers saw it as an act of nature, a punishment no less, for
perceived indolence amongst the farmers. I knew better of course
and begged the hunters to set out and kill the pack. They refused
and it seemed to me that they would simply dwindle, vanishing
one by one every night until there was nobody left alive in the place
but the fleet of foot or the unappetising.

"I interfered. To do so is to break a cardinal rule amongst those
like me who make it their life's mission to see the world and the
varying cultures it offers. Still, I could not stand by and see more
die. I saw the weeping parents, trying to remain strong in the eyes
of the god they decided had seen fit to punish them, and knew that
I could not just stand by.

"I tracked the wolf pack over a period of two days." He took a
calm sip of his tea. "No more children died at their hands."

"And yet," Holmes said, "it could be said that nature was simply
taking its course, the weak feeding the strong."

"Survival of the fittest," Carruthers said. "Whether my Remington
could be deemed unnatural or not I think I proved myself fit
enough."

Holmes nodded. "I don't disapprove," he said, "just thinking
aloud. Darwinism haunts our steps in these matters. I find myself
thinking more and more about what this research could bring.
Is man wrong to interfere in the passage of so-called natural law
or is he simply exhibiting the intelligent dominance that proves
the validity of that law? As the dominant species can we not be
expected to become stronger and stronger until there is nothing
that can harm us? And what then? Where does it all lead? What

manner of creature are humans destined to become?"

"Well," said Carruthers, "if you want my opinion, lonely ones. We can't seem to bear sharing our world, not with other animals, not with other humans for that matter. If we don't sort that little flaw out then one day there'll be nothing left of this planet but a spinning, empty rock."

"Oh now," I said, "surely we're not as bad as all that? Mankind can be capable of great kindnesses and consideration. We're not the voracious destroyers you think."

"But those who are outnumber those who aren't," he replied. "And I fear they will not stop until they've ravaged our world. But then –" he smiled over the ridge of his teacup as he drained it "– if we don't deal with this Moreau fellow, there might not even be much left of the world to ravage!"

"Sir?" said a waiter at Holmes' arm. "Are you Mr Sherlock Holmes?"

"I am indeed," he replied, taking a telegram from the proffered silver platter.

"How on earth could anyone know you were here?" I asked.

"There's only one man I would rely on to pull such a trick," he said, opening the telegram.

"Mycroft," I agreed with a chuckle.

Holmes did not share my good humour. In fact his face was positively ashen as he lowered the telegram. "Gentlemen," he said, "I fear we may have left it too long to act. A man calling himself Dr Moreau appeared at the Houses of Parliament an hour ago."

"He's been captured?" asked Carruthers.

"Far from it," Holmes replied. "He's abducted the Prime Minister!"

PART FOUR

THE PIG-HEADED VILLAIN

CHAPTER TWENTY-EIGHT

All three of us made our way to the Diogenes Club. This time the meeting would take place on Mycroft's territory, the silent and smoky hallways of which were more than simply a gentlemen's club.

The Diogenes is often discussed as the strictest and most unfriendly club in the city. Its members, some of the most influential and important men in the land, are forbidden to speak except in certain isolated areas. It prides itself on homing the most unclubbable men in the country, men so anti-social and misanthropic that no other building would have them. Of course this has the effect of making many people wish to join, there is nothing quite so attractive to a certain stratum of society as exclusivity, even if that exclusivity is earned at the cost of their social reputation. But few were allowed to join the club, the board saw to that.

The board was composed of one man, the same man that had established the club so as to have a central office within which to conduct his business: Mycroft Holmes. The club had become an extension of his secret empire, a place filled with those with real power. Not the Cabinet, which was in Mycroft's view nothing more than an ever-shifting selection of public functionaries, rather than long-term men of money and position. Those who supported the Cabinet; who provided the leverage and finance to see things get done. In many ways the Diogenes *was* the government, the quietly beating heart at its centre that kept the country afloat. And now, in this state of emergency, that heart was beating harder than ever.

"Good morning, Gentlemen," said the footman who greeted us at the doorway. "Mr Holmes is expecting you." He led us up the stairs to the front door. "Need I remind you that, even in these trying times, the rules of the club stand. Once we are beyond those doors you are to say nothing until you are within the visitors' room."

"Nothing?" asked Carruthers, a man to whom this sort of behaviour was an anathema.

"Absolutely nothing, Sir," the footman confirmed. "Failure to observe this rule will result in one of the staff ejecting you from the premises."

"And we wouldn't want that," said Holmes. "I'm sure Carruthers has been thrown out of much better clubs than this in his time, after all."

"Well, actually, I was once banned from the Coleman but that was entirely down to a misunderstanding with regards a demonstration of Chinese wrestling. I got a bit carried away and threw a member of staff through a picture window. It was quite a scandal at the time."

"No doubt," I said.

We were ushered through the front door into the charge of another member of staff, this one even more aged than the last. He had the face of a baby bird, a bulbous cranium surrounded by straggling hair with a nose that looked more than up to the task of fishing a snail from its shell. He gave a deferential nod that turned into a panicked shake as Carruthers opened his mouth to greet him. I nudged the garrulous explorer in the ribs and was relieved to see he got the hint. He adopted a music-hall routine of mime, rolling his eyes, slapping his wrist and making buttoning gestures at his lips.

The bird-faced gentleman led us up the giant staircase to the fourth floor of the club. I often wondered if the visitors' areas were located on the top floor as an extra deterrent against sociability. Certainly there was little Mycroft would dread more than climbing all those stairs. He would never make the journey unless it was absolutely unavoidable.

We were led into the main visitors' room where Mycroft sat in the window observing the street outside. Whenever I had met him here this was the position he adopted. I realise now that it was his version of that walk Holmes and I had conducted through the city. It was Mycroft's opportunity to remind himself what the real world – and all the people in it – were really like.

"Well," he said, without turning around, "I don't imagine any of us thought matters would come to a head as quickly as this."

"Indeed not," Holmes agreed standing at Mycroft's side and gazing through the glass at the street below. "Tell us what happened."

"The Prime Minister was addressing the House of Lords on the matter of Ireland," Mycroft sighed, "as he so often does. It was neither a particularly heated debate nor an important one, just the usual hot air that keeps that building warm through the winter months.

"Moreau – or whoever he is – gained access through the cellars. We later found a hole knocked through from one of the expanded train tunnels." He looked up for the first time. "We're having our own station built as part of the Underground network, saves time all round. Anyway, once inside the building he made his way to the main debating chamber. He was not alone."

"He had some of his creations with him?" asked Holmes.

Mycroft nodded. "According to one of the security officers there was a gang of eight, all of them recognisable as different animal species. A leopard, a goat, a… dear Lord… a horse! Oh, damn it all it was positively a bloody farmyard! And he played the part, he wore a pig's face as a mask."

"Really? That is interesting."

"It's damned grotesque. Obviously the majority assumed they were all wearing masks, then one of the damned things spoke and the way its mouth moved…"

"We have seen something of a similar nature," Holmes said, briefly describing our encounter with Kane. "This security officer, might we hear the story direct from him?"

Mycroft nodded and gestured towards the old member of staff. "I thought you might ask that. Bring him in, Kirk."

Kirk led in a small, stocky fellow who looked like he was completely out of his environment. Some people are simply more physical than others and this fellow looked like he was probably snapping the floorboards simply by standing on them.

"Fellowes, Sir," he announced, holding out a worn, strong hand that looked all too capable of crushing the bones of mine to powder.

"Dr John Watson," I replied, shaking the man's hand.

"A pleasure to meet another old soldier," he said. "I was wounded out around the same time as yourself. Good to finally put a face to the name."

Mycroft was quick to cut the regimental reunions short. "We haven't time for all the pleasantries, Fellowes," he said. "Kindly explain to my brother exactly what happened."

"Of course, Sir," said Fellowes, clearly not in the least bit discomfited by the mild rebuke. A man who worked with politicians no doubt developed a thick skin to such things.

"As Mr Holmes has probably told you, our first assumption was that we faced a group of terrorists. It wouldn't be the first time some group or another decided to storm the building and grind their axe in public. Normally they're easily dealt with. These groups may have a good deal of enthusiasm but they have no training and that's what really counts in the end, as Dr Watson here will attest I'm sure."

"Absolutely," I said, completely on impulse. Fellowes was the sort of man that could make you agree just by being in the same room as him. He had a very powerful personality.

"Given their bizarre mode of dress my first assumption was the animal rights lot, you know, anti-vivisection and what have you."

"Quite the opposite, if anything," said Mycroft waving his hands at Fellowes to encourage him to continue.

"Speaking personally, it was the horse-headed feller that first convinced me we were dealing with more than just a bunch of mutters in masks," Fellowes continued. "He spoke up you see, told Sir Bartleby of the Exchequer to shut his face (the honourable gentleman was doing more than his fair share of screaming you see, Sirs). The way he opened his mouth was more than a theatrical costumier could manage and that was a fact. I saw its teeth, tongue and throat and knew that what I was looking at was a horse's head on a bloke's body. Absolutely ludicrous, naturally, but I've seen a fair few ludicrous things in my time and if there's one thing

I've learned working security it's that you should never stop to question the obvious. I couldn't begin to tell you how you got a horse's head stitched onto a fellow but as I was looking right at one, somebody surely had managed and there was little to be gained by questioning it. The brute had designs on a number of peers, peers that fell under my care. So – figure out the how and why of it later – in that moment you just get on and do your job.

"Not that I was able to do much of that – those things had the strength to match their ugliness and I can honestly say that man was not built to punch horses." He held up a bandaged right hand. "Made a right mess of me hand it did."

"The chief was the odd one out – his face weren't a part of him, however much he might have wished it were, snorting and oinking like the poor swine that had owned the face before him. It was a rough, butcher's-shop job, hollowed out and worn like a cowl, the ears flapping as he shouted his orders. He looked an idiot to be honest but the gun in his hand probably went a fair way towards convincing people not to mention it.

"I'm embarrassed to say they had our number within seconds. I'm not blaming the men, they didn't know what they were looking at. They had the wind blown out of them and it made them slow to react. Still, like I say, training – that's what you need. If they'd been a bit more like me they'd have got the job done and not worried about what they were beating up.

"Once you're on your back foot though it's usually too late. Situation like that you've got to keep the upper hand from the off, otherwise they'll make their move, grab hostages or what have you, and from there on you're trying to limit the damage rather than win the day.

"That's what happened to us, they grabbed Lord Bartleby, Lord Messingham and Lord Wharburton. The three of them were on their knees, looking death in the face before we could even rally a proper defence. Of course, had I known what they had in mind I dare say I would have taken the risk anyway. Without wishing to dismiss the worth of those noble gentlemen…"

"You'd rather risk an old peer than a Prime Minister," said Holmes.

"That's it, Sir," said Fellowes, "you've got it.

"But I didn't know of course so I was shouting for people to stand down before we ended up spilling blood that we'd struggle to mop up.

"Pig-face took up the speaker's position and made his little speech. I'll give it to you as verbatim as I can, Gentlemen, I can't say it meant a great deal to me but I've been doing this game long enough to know that details are important so I do my best to keep everything locked away." He tapped the side of his head.

"He said: 'This is an action on behalf of the army of Dr Moreau.' I remembered the name but couldn't think why at the time. Since then I've placed it of course. Outside the heat of the moment there's not much that escapes this ugly old head of mine.

"'For too long, this world has been under the control of the stupid apes,' he carried on, which was a bit rich considering one of his men had a monkey's face on him. But, there you go, you don't expect much in the way of sense from a man who wears a pig's head as a mask, do you?

"'I am here,' he said, 'to take away that control and place it in the hands of the next species, the better species. Mankind has had its chance and proven itself incapable time and time again.'

"He got a real good rant going then but I'm afraid I missed a lot of it. That pig mask of his obscured his words something chronic, and when he got excited all you could hear was the sound of wind being forced through that dead old snout of his. It was something of a one-sided history lesson, from The Hundred Years' War to the Boers – anything and everything he could think to moan about with regard our track record. Personally I think it's all too easy to give mankind a bad name as long as you're happy to be selective, we've all done things we're not proud of.

"Anyway, it wasn't the speech of a sane man so I don't know why I bother trying to judge it. The man was a loon and a dangerous one at that.

"One of my boys decided to try and take his opportunity while pig-face was orating to the masses. He made a break for the doors; I like to think he was rushing to fetch help rather than just thinking about his own neck but we'll never know. One of the creatures, the leopard-headed one, jumped for him. I tell you, it wasn't just his head that was unnatural, that thing leaped feet into the air, sailing over people's heads, before landing on the poor lad. Its teeth made short work of him. He was nothing but bone above the neck by the time he'd taken a couple of bites.

"Of course that soon made the room panic, there was no more time for speeches. The Lords were shouting and screaming and pushing each other out of the way. At the sight of all this chaos the animals were quick to join in too, they were barking and screeching and leaping all over the place. It was only pig-face, Moreau, that managed to get them back on side. 'Fear the Law!' he started shouting, 'Fear the Law!'

"Well, they hadn't been doing much of that had they? Still, they gathered round him quick enough so it had the desired effect. Of course the rest of us were not so organised. It was madness in there as people made a break for the doors. It took them a few minutes to realise that nothing was stopping them. Moreau had used the chaos to grab the Prime Minister and make his escape. I'm afraid I didn't even see him do it, it was only afterwards, when cross-examining those who were there that we realised what had happened.

"The Prime Minister had been making for the exit the same as everyone else but the horse-headed one and a short, hairy thing that had a good dose of goat in him had snatched at him before he'd got so much as a few feet across the hall. According to the Speaker of the House, they put a sack over his head and the horse creature carried him out under one arm. The man in question claims he tried to intercede on the Prime Minister's behalf but, honestly, I don't believe a word of it, I think he was as scared as all the rest and making it up after the fact as he didn't want to be seen as a coward. Frankly there'd be no shame in what he did, he's an old man and he's never seen active service. No reason why he should suddenly become the man of action when faced with that sort of thing."

"And they left the building the same way?" asked Holmes.

"They did, gone into the tunnels before we could get any kind of party together.

"I investigated some way down there myself but it soon became obvious that I had no chance of pursuing them in the dark, not on my own anyway. In these sorts of situations it's never long before we receive communication. If they've taken the Prime Minister then likely they want a ransom, we'll soon hear how much and what they expect us to do next."

"That may be so," said Mycroft, "but I'd rather not wait for them to make the next move, not if we can help it."

"We most certainly can help it," said Holmes, "we make our move tonight!"

CHAPTER TWENTY-NINE

Once Fellowes had been shown from the room, Mycroft turned to his brother.

"You seem particularly confident, Sherlock," he said. "Do you really think Kane intends to lead you to Moreau's base of operations?"

"I'm fairly certain we'll have matters resolved before the night is out," Holmes replied.

"That, my brother, is not quite what I asked."

Holmes merely smiled. "This has not been a case to exercise the brain, Mycroft, as biologically fascinating as some of its details may have been, the matter was a simple enough one. Now it simply comes down to fast action."

He turned to me. "Watson, we need to gather a hunting party, would you be so good as to visit The British Museum and enlist Professor Challenger? Of the lot of them he's the least likely to fall dead of shock the minute he enters the sewers."

"Nothing could kill that man," said Mycroft. "He has the sensitivity of an ox."

"Just so," Holmes agreed. "And however much Kane may wish it otherwise we simply must have police involvement."

Mycroft shifted in his seat. "I would rather this wasn't the talk of Scotland Yard, Holmes. Is there really any need to drag one of your tame inspectors into this?"

"I would trust Lestrade to be discreet," Holmes replied. "Gregson too, but both are far too well known within the city, I have no doubt Kane would recognise them."

"Perhaps he just needs to accept that not everything can be as he wishes it," I suggested. I was more than happy at the idea of the creature being taken down a peg or two. I disliked pandering to him in the least.

"As much as it irritates me to admit it, Watson, we need him. I may have talked a good game at Baker Street but he is in a much stronger position than we are and he's clever enough to know it. The minute Lestrade turns up on the doorstep, Kane is likely to be out of the back window and halfway up the street.

"Ultimately, what does Kane care if these experiments continue? Oh, he has an axe to grind, of that I'm sure, he wishes for revenge, but he desires his continued freedom even more."

"That's if he even intends to help us at all. It must have occurred to you that this could be a trap?"

"Certainly, most probably sprung with his creator's knowledge. If he wanted to kill us after all, he could have achieved that easily enough back at Baker Street..."

"He nearly did."

Holmes smiled. "Just so. So why is he keeping us alive? It is either because he is still too scared of his creator to countenance facing him alone, he wants us to help him destroy him, or he is still working for the man he calls his father and his entire story is nothing but a tissue of deceit."

"There's one sure way to find out," said Mycroft.

"Indeed," said Holmes, "but we must at least allow ourselves some chance of success!"

A thought had occurred to me. "I know just the man!" I said. "Inspector Mann, he's not local but he's certainly trustworthy."

I looked to Mycroft who reluctantly nodded. "I'll just have to trust your judgement, Doctor," he said. "But Heaven help you if this ends up in *The Police Gazette*."

"Excellent," Holmes agreed, "I leave you to contact him. I have another couple of fellows in mind but I shall drop a line to them on my way."

"On your way where?" I asked, only too aware that I was being left out of the picture again.

"To the home address of the man claiming to be Dr Moreau," he said, "with whatever representatives of the law Mycroft will allow me."

"What?" Both Mycroft and I asked the same question. Neither of us could believe what Holmes had said.

"Oh I don't expect him to be there," Holmes said, as if that explained everything to everyone's possible satisfaction. "The man's not an idiot, and while he has done everything possible to cover his identity, I sincerely doubt he'll risk capture at this important stage in his plans."

"But who is it?" I asked.

Holmes just smiled. "After your excellent work on this case I wouldn't dream of telling you. You'll come to the same conclusion

I'm sure, and feel all the more vindicated to have done so under your own steam."

I could have throttled him.

"And what about me?" asked Carruthers. "What would you like me to do? I'd hate not to be of service at this important stage in the case."

"Mr Carruthers," said Holmes, "the role you play will be of vital importance, rest assured of that."

He looked at me. "Please, Watson, we haven't much time! Challenger! Mann!"

I considered arguing but experience had taught me how efficacious that usually was. "Very well," I said, "I shall be your errand boy."

With considerable restraint I managed to walk out of the room and through the rest of the building without making a single noise.

CHAPTER THIRTY

I cannot recall ever feeling as despondent about my relationship with Holmes as I did during the journey between the Diogenes Club and The British Museum. Certainly there had been many times when Holmes and I had failed to see eye to eye; I had been the target for considerable insults and slights over the years. But there had always been an underlying respect between us, an understanding that, for all his bluster and unreasonable behaviour, the two of us were a partnership. Now, for all his guff about my wanting to come to my own conclusions, all I could see was that I was being deliberately sidelined. He would tell me nothing and, to add further insult, he would not even involve me in the important aspects of the case.

In all honesty I felt like leaving Baker Street just as I had those few years ago, not to take up a new life as had been the case then, but simply to eradicate the irritations of the current one.

I had the cab stop at a telegraph office en route, glad at least that I had been able to bring Inspector Mann into the fold. I was aware of how my attitude towards the policeman's feelings was the direct opposite of those of Holmes. I wanted to show Mann trust and respect, I wanted him to be involved rather than stuck on the periphery. I wanted to offer him the things I most wanted for myself. We are very simple creatures, are we not? Whatever the alienists say, the human mind is usually pretty predictable.

I arrived at The British Museum and was relieved at the ease with which I was able to pass through the door; arriving during its hours of opening made things a lot easier. Of course, I was naive to think that I would simply be able to stroll right into the Reading Room where the Science Club had taken up residence.

"Ah, is that Dr Watson?" asked an elderly voice. My heart sank to see the ageing caretaker sat in a chair outside the Reading Room door.

"Indeed it is," I replied, determined to keep my voice cheery.

He carefully placed a wilting sandwich back into its brown paper nest on his lap, treating it with all the reverence you would expect were it an exhibit. It certainly looked old enough to be. "I'll be the judge of that," he said, once sure it was safe in his lap. "I am a highly contagious, respiration-borne virus. I can lead to pneumonia, bronchitis, encephalitis and ear infections. Fifty years ago I wiped out nearly half the population of Hawaii. What am I?"

I knew damn well what he was but was raised far too well to shout it in public. I therefore had little choice but to answer his question instead.

"Measles," I replied, "otherwise known as 'rubeola'. Now may I go in or do you wish to give me a physical examination first to make sure I haven't got any?"

"No need to be like that, Doctor," he replied, picking up his sandwich once more and offering up a particularly floppy corner to his wrinkled mouth. "We all have our role to play after all."

And there he had a point – given how I had been bemoaning my involvement, how much worse would it have been to be this man? Sitting in doorways and knowing nothing but arguments and grumpy general practitioners. Still, he didn't have to be such an unbearable prig about it.

I stepped inside to see the Science Club indulging in their usual chaos. Perry had fallen asleep amongst the book stacks, Cavor appeared to be trying to fold a rug into the shape of a typical paper dart, and Lindenbrook was drawing on the back of a bookshelf with some chalk. It seemed inconceivable to me that anything worthwhile could come out of such an obvious collection of lunatics. Later, Mycroft would admit that he paid the cleaner to gather all notes (copying those left on non-portable surfaces such as walls and floors) and hired a team of scientists to decipher their content. Apparently, by so doing, he has blueprints for an improved combustion engine, an entirely new number and the likely outcome of every single cricket match played at Lord's cricket ground for the next three years – eclectic information, certainly, but groundbreaking nonetheless.

Of Challenger there was, irritatingly, no sign.

"Professor?" I called.

"Get down man!" came the man's familiar roar and I dropped to the floor as a native spear passed through the space where I had just been standing and imbedded itself in the spine of *Litefoot's Lepidoptera volume three, E-G.*

"I nearly had you then!" the professor laughed, bounding through the tables, another large spear in his hand. "I often find physical exercise keeps the brain firing!" he said, as if that was a perfectly adequate explanation. "I have been giving thought to the question of how waxing the feathers can improve the wind resistance."

I might have suggested that he had enough to think about without branching out into the aerodynamics of pointed weaponry, but I was concerned he'd stab me with the other spear if I did. With Challenger no response was impossible. Instead, I brought him up to date with the investigation and extended Holmes' offer for him to join us on the night's mission.

"An expedition!" Challenger exclaimed. "What a splendid idea!" He leaned close. "And if nothing else it will get me away from these idiots!"

Looking over his shoulder, I could see that Cavor was climbing into his upholstered dart, looking for all the world as if he intended to try and fly it out of the building. Perry gave a loud snore, woke himself up and fell over in a cloud of tumbling books.

"I can see why that would appeal," I said. "We'll see you at Baker Street at eight, then?"

"I shall be there!"

CHAPTER THIRTY-ONE

Stepping out onto Great Russell Street, I wondered quite what to do with myself. As far as I knew, Holmes was, at that very minute, poking through the evidence at the home of the man he knew to be "Moreau". Given my absence, the last thing I fancied doing was returning to our rooms and waiting there like a dutiful wife.

I was furious, walking down the street, banging the paving stones with my cane. I would have given anything to have Holmes there, I would have given him a piece of my mind that even he, in his cold and logical way, would struggle to dismiss.

How dare he be so patronising! I would come to the same conclusion, and would feel more vindicated by coming to it under my own steam, would I?

Well, I dare say I could come to the same conclusion. As much as Holmes liked to paint me the idiot, it was a distinctly uncharitable impression. I might not have the same skills as he did, the same leaning towards deduction and the interpretation of data, but that didn't make me a dullard. We had already decided that there was a limit to who could continue Moreau's work, either the man himself or someone who had worked closely with him. From what Holmes had said then it was clear that he didn't believe the culprit to be Moreau himself. That was logical enough. Even if we ignored Prendick's statement that the man had been torn limb from limb he would be decrepit by now, and the rampaging pig-faced man did not sound like a fellow in his dotage. So we were left with the people who worked with him. Those who studied his methods well enough to be able to duplicate and continue them. So, Prendick or Montgomery, both of whom were also apparently dead, the former to the satisfaction of a police inspector whose opinion I had trusted enough to consider the matter a fact. So what about Montgomery, the drunk, the sometime employee of Mycroft's Department?

As I walked I became increasingly unaware of my direction. I was simply marching the streets, powering my thoughts with the urgent pounding of my feet.

Ideas were flooding through my head, random words and phrases, mental images. I saw Prendick's mad writing on the wall of his home: *Fear the Law!* – the phrase uttered by "Moreau" when wishing to bring his animal army under control at the Houses of Parliament; repeated by Moreau's creatures on the island, according to Prendick's manuscript. I thought of that single copy of *The Times* and the pile of copies of *The Chronicle* he had kept. That made me pause. I actually stopped stock-still in the street. It didn't make sense. If he normally read *The Chronicle* then why had he received a copy of *The Times*? Had that been sent to him as a threat? Most likely. And what of the religious pamphlet with its bizarre quote? Was that relevant?

I took Prendick's manuscript from my pocket and flicked through the last few pages. People had to veer around me, tutting and moaning at the distracted man who stood in the middle of the street reading sheets of paper. I barely noticed them as I skimmed through the climax of his report. I read of Moreau's death and suddenly a piece of the jigsaw fell into place.

"'Children of the Law,'" I read aloud, quoting Prendick's words as he faced Moreau's creatures after the man's death. Prendick was scared of them, convinced that they would turn on him and Montgomery unless he persuaded them to stay true to the dead man's principles, Moreau's "religion". "He is not dead," Prendick had continued. "He has changed his shape – he has changed his body... For a time you will not see him. He is... there." At this point in his account, Prendick describes how he pointed to the sky, suggesting Moreau's elevation to the divine, "where he can watch you. You cannot see him. But he can see you." Then that phrase again, "Fear the Law."

These were familiar words of course, copied onto that religious pamphlet, along with the newspaper, the trigger that had driven Prendick to suicide.

But who had sent them? Montgomery? It must be – he was the only man left to have worked with Moreau...

And then it hit me, and those sheets of Prendick's manuscript fluttered from my hands as I realised what I had been missing all along. Montgomery was not the only other man to have worked with Moreau. There was another. One who would have had easy access to Prendick's statement when he had first returned from the South Pacific, who would have found it only too easy to trace him and send him a copy of a newspaper and a veiled threat. There was one man who had hidden in plain sight throughout the whole affair. Knowing it – and like Holmes has said in the past, even without proof I did *know* it, it was nothing less than a fact to me – the sense of unity that washed over my mind was incredible. For all his loathsome behaviour, Holmes had been quite right, in that to have come to the realisation myself was something that quite simply took my breath away. I knew who had been behind it all.

It was something of a surprise to find he was climbing out of a carriage and walking across the road towards me.

"Hello Doctor," said Mitchell. "I've been hunting for you ever since my operatives told me you were leaving The British Museum."

"You!" I said, still somewhat in shock, both at my own realisation of the identity of the new "Moreau" and the fact that he was now right here in front of me. "All that time you helped him, undercover, writing your story, all that time, damning him in public, ensuring he was hounded out of the country… all that time…"

"I was thinking what I might gain from such fascinating work, yes," Mitchell said. "But here is not the place for such conversations." He gestured towards the driver of the carriage, who stepped down and walked slowly towards us. His bowler hat was pulled low, a muffler covering most of his face. But when he came right up to me I found I was looking directly into the eyes of a cat. The driver tugged the muffler down slightly, enough to reveal the shiny black skin and snarling fangs of a panther.

"I have need of your company," said Mitchell. "Please don't be so stupid as to refuse. My friend here could take your head off with one swipe of his arm."

I had no doubt this was true. No doubt this was the very beast that had so viciously savaged Fellowes' security officer.

"What do you want from me?" I asked, as the driver took hold of my arm and pulled me towards the carriage.

"Oh, a little leverage," said Mitchell, following behind us, "and a man can never have too many living specimens to work on."

As I was yanked into the darkness of the carriage, he stepped in behind me, and his smile was as animalistic as any of his creations'. "Just you wait until you see what I can make of you!"

PART FIVE

INTO THE LION'S DEN

CHAPTER THIRTY-TWO

I am only too aware that, having criticised Watson's handling of my case notes, I am now in a decidedly precarious position. Though hardly so precarious as Watson, kidnapped from the street and at the mercy of a mad man and his terrifying menagerie.

As for whether I can satisfy his imaginary readers – of this, a case that will likely never be read – only time will tell. Certainly, I can do no worse. If his editor ever has cause to read it and is concerned that it is lacking in excitement I hereby give my permission for him to insert a superfluous boat chase or fist fight. I trust that what few intelligent readers my Boswell has left will have the good sense to skip such juvenilia and move straight on to the facts.

I must confess, the conclusion of the Moreau affair was somewhat tedious. From that point on it was little more than battles with inhumane monsters beneath the streets of London, none of the really interesting cerebral problems that feature in my better cases. Watson rarely talks about those, the affair of the Doomsday Book

Murder for example, a conundrum solved entirely in repose on my chaise longue – fourteen hours of the most thrilling mental arithmetic, logical deduction and abstract contemplation. One day I shall write it up myself, as a beautifully cold and precise novel. It shall be the pinnacle account of my career.

But, for now, let us cover up our agonised boredom and talk of monsters and madmen.

CHAPTER THIRTY-THREE

But I dash ahead of myself (no doubt in apathetic determination to have the matter done). First there was the examination of Mitchell's house.

I had no doubt that Watson would soon realise that Mitchell was our man. After all, it was by far the most obvious solution. While Moreau had published frequently he had obviously never put pen to paper on the subject of creating animal hybrids. Whoever the current perpetrator was, he clearly modelled himself after Moreau and yet wished to preserve his anonymity (the pig's mask could have simply been Grand Guignol but I was willing to bet that it was a practical consideration too). Therefore we were after someone who was known to us who had had direct experience working with Moreau. Of the four people to match that description, three of them were dead. It was hardly a complex conclusion to reach.

But why? That question still stood. An answer to that and a possible clue as to the location of his laboratory (for only a fool would entirely pin their hopes on a vicious criminal with the head of a dog) drew me to investigate Mitchell's home.

Mycroft commanded Fellowes to accompany me. This was somewhat irritating as the man insisted on talking despite having nothing more to say. Trying to think clearly next to such a source of endless noise is like trying to play the violin next to a dynamite explosion. It was a long and irksome journey.

"Here we are," I announced in relief as we reached Mitchell's home. Fellowes had been talking about his favourite music-hall tunes, a phrase I considered an oxymoron, so the timing couldn't have been better, as I had spent the last few minutes in mortal fear that he might begin singing some of them.

The house was part of a small terrace, one of those dreary suburban properties that clog up our city, the sort of place clerks live.

"Mitchell will have long gone," I said to Fellowes as we walked up the front path. "He will have left shortly after Watson's visit. Knowing that we were investigating the matter he will have known we would return to his doorstep soon enough, only an idiot would sit and wait for such an eventuality."

Fellowes reached for the door handle. "Will we need to force our way in?" he asked.

I put a hand on his arm. "Perhaps, but let us proceed with caution, it would not be beyond Mitchell's skills to have left a trap for us."

Fellowes tried the handle. "It's not locked," he said, pushing the door open gently.

I hooked my cane around his arm and pulled him back from the doorway. "All the more reason to assume there's danger," I insisted. "Mitchell is making it as easy as possible for us."

Fellowes nodded. For all his verbal diarrhoea he was a professional when it came to security. "Stand well back then, Sir," he said, "and keep out of the direct line of the doorway."

I had already done as much, naturally. I once had a suspect prepare a catapult of broken glass behind his office door, determined to shred the face of his pursuer should they visit. Luckily for me he was as competent a layer of traps as he was an embezzler. Lestrade was left to pick up the pieces when the trap triggered early, spraying the inside of the room with its load.

The door opened and nothing came flying out at us.

Fellowes, still inclined to caution, inched towards the doorway and looked to the floor for signs of a tripwire.

"It's dark in there," he said, "but there is something…"

There was a loud hissing noise and Fellowes fell back, a viper darting at his face.

"Keep back!" I shouted, leaping forward and lashing out with my cane.

The serpent was not alone, a nest of them thrashed wildly just inside the door, mouths wide open, fangs bared.

"Something's riled them," said Fellowes, now standing at my shoulder. "They're nervous things normally. Saw my fair share of them in India – the tail-end of one anyway, as it vanished into the brush."

The snakes darted for the doorway, and Fellowes and I had no choice but to beat and stamp at them with our feet, better that than let them escape out into the street where they could bite some unfortunate passer-by.

"If we'd walked right in…" said Fellowes.

"Then we would have been bitten several times over," I added.

I sniffed the air and noted a chemical tang I was familiar with. Looking at the door I could see a line of twine extending from the top of it to the door-jamb, then extending out into the gloom of the entrance hall.

Fellowes stepped inside, a lit match in his hands. "We need more light on the subject," he announced, lighting the gas lamps.

"Careful!" I shouted, one last snake uncurling from the bracket of a wall sconce.

"Damn it!" he shouted, pulling back his hands in alarm. "Nearly had me then."

He took my cane and tugged the snake from the light fitting. "Nasty little brutes," he said as he brought his boot down on its head.

"Cottonmouth snakes," I explained, "from North America. They are mean-spirited in their natural environment but these were encouraged. When you opened the door you pulled that string…" I said, pointing at where it was tacked along the wall. At the far end of the hallway stood a large wooden case, its trapdoor open and a glass beaker up-ended inside it. "The string tugged the trapdoor open which in turn tipped a beaker of what smells like formic acid onto the serpents."

"No wonder they were in a bad mood."

"'No wonder,' indeed. They would naturally have lashed out."

"Aye," said Fellowes looking at the dead snakes with some guilt, "them and me both."

"It can't be helped," I said, cautiously opening another doorway off the hall.

"You sure you want to do that?" asked Fellowes. "Probably a pack of tigers in there."

I opened the door. It led onto a small sitting room, with dusty chairs, an ill-kempt rug, and a long-cold fire grate. I estimated the room hadn't been used for about fourteen weeks (give or take a few days). But then Mitchell was not likely to have entertained many guests.

"There is nothing here to interest us," I said, and moved to the next door.

Opening this, I was faced with an entirely different sight. This had been Mitchell's study, the room where he had met Watson.

"Check the other rooms," I told Fellowes, to get him out from underneath my feet. "But be careful in case he has left any more specimens to greet us."

"Righto," he said, and began a slow circuit of the house.

Mitchell's desk was virtually empty. A single sheet of paper was placed in its centre, like a portrait framed in a wide mount, to offer emphasis.

I picked the sheet of paper up, not entirely surprised to note that it was a letter addressed to me:

My dear Mr Holmes,

Sorry to have missed you but it was clear to me that if you were investigating it could only be a matter of time before you came knocking on my door. I flatter myself that I caused no suspicion in the mind of your colleague, Dr Watson, but am not so confident that I could manage the same with you. Your reputation is, after all, somewhat daunting.

It is no great imposition to leave. This has become my second home of late now my work grows apace. And what work it is! You will soon see what I am capable of, and not just me but the countless other species we share this planet with. For too long, mankind has forgotten its place in the animal kingdom, Mr Holmes, we have forgotten that we are no more than another species of mammal, another mouth to feed on this packed Earth. We think we rule, but only because we have stamped out every other creature, choked it with our smoke and poison, buried it beneath our tarmac and brick. The richness that we have destroyed, Mr Holmes, the diversity that is lost to us – it is a crime greater than any of the petty affairs you have turned your attention to over the years.

But fear not, I am intending to redress that balance. I have learned from one of the greatest enemies of animal-kind, that abuser, that false god, Moreau. His methods are now turned against his intentions. He wanted to subjugate other species even further, make them work our factories, clean our streets, fight our wars. Well, they will fight, indeed they will, but the Army of Dr Moreau is not one he could ever have imagined, it is a force that will put the arrogant humans in their place once and for all. We are the future, Holmes. We are tomorrow. Fear the Law!

Yours,
Albert Mitchell

"What have you got there?" Fellowes asked, having finished his tour of the house. "Anything useful?"

I handed it to him. "In the sense that it supplies motive," I said. "It never fails to irritate me that the things that will always obfuscate an investigation are the peculiarities of the human mind. How difficult it is to predict, how impossible to plan against when it will not follow a logical pattern."

Fellowes handed the letter back. "Sounds nutty as a fruitcake to me."

"My point precisely." I put the letter in my pocket and began a more thorough search of the office. Mad or not, Mitchell was not stupid; there was no evidence that could lead us to his underground lair.

"Show me the bedroom," I asked.

"Righto."

Fellowes led me through to Mitchell's chamber and I spent some time investigating the soles of his boots and the cuffs of his trousers. They were at least of some use, showing me several distinct mud traces that narrowed matters down. Still it was not enough.

"Nothing?" Fellowes asked.

"Nothing," I conceded. "There is only one way to proceed. Straight into the lion's den."

CHAPTER THIRTY-FOUR

I sent Fellowes off to report to Mycroft and returned to Baker Street expecting to find Watson, no doubt livid with irritation at my behaviour. Instead I found two other gentlemen entirely.

"Johnson!" I said. "You got my message then, I was concerned that it would arrive too late."

"Nah, Mr Holmes, I got it all right, and I were only too happy to come, weren't I?"

"Same goes for me," said the other fellow, jumping to his feet and standing before me, nervously wringing his cap between his hands. I'm afraid he has a habit of that sort of thing. He has grown up to be somewhat in awe. Only natural of course, I was a dominant force in his childhood and inspired him to his current trade.

"Wiggins?" I said. "Good to see you, I heard of your success in finding the stolen ruby of Balmoor, congratulations!"

"It was a simple enough case, Mr Holmes, I'm sure you would have made short work of it."

"No doubt," I admitted, choosing not to mention that the location of the gem and the identity of its thief had been clear to me by the time I was halfway through reading *The Times*' coverage of its loss.

Wiggins was a graduate of my Baker Street Irregulars. In fact he had always been their guiding hand, the others had looked up to him just as he had looked up to me.

For some time I had suspected he might consider a career in the police force, his enthusiasm for detective work was clear and I never doubted it was something that would continue to develop as he grew older. Thankfully he decided against such a mundane expression of his abilities and became a private agent instead.

One of the more predictable effects of Watson's writings has been the burgeoning industry of independent detectives. They have always existed of course, merrily pandering to the public's inane confusions with their limited skills. They were something I was quick to distance myself from, classing myself as a "consulting" detective, one that helped the official police force rather than just the braying public. Still, after my methods became so well known and my successes so widely discussed, the business of deduction became a boom industry. (I also believe the name "Sherlock" found a brief popularity amongst expectant mothers for which I can only apologise to the infants in question.) Private investigators sprung up all over the country ranging from large-scale operations with a sizeable staff to individual operators working out of their own parlours. It seemed that everyone had suddenly developed a skill for deduction and wanted nothing more than to share it. I had no doubt that the majority of such organisations were an exercise in wish-fulfilment and their owners would be out of business before the ink dried on their business cards.

If any private individual stood a chance at making a go of it though, it would be Wiggins, and I for one was pleased to see him try. I realised it might be appreciated were I to suggest as much to him. (I often forget these personal details when Watson is absent.)

"I was considerably impressed," I told him, thinking the words through carefully, "and have no doubt that great things stand ahead of you." I sat down in a vacant armchair. "That's as long as you manage to survive the night of course."

"I dare say all of us will have our work cut out managing that," said Johnson, "but then, I never did take to the quiet life."

"Dr Watson not here?" asked Wiggins.

"Not as yet," I admitted. "No doubt he is sulking somewhere as he is wont to do. We'll see him soon enough. Let me give you both some idea of what faces us."

I prepared to give them all the details currently at our disposal. My brother might have wished me to show more discretion but knowledge is the most important thing in the world and I wouldn't dream of letting them go into battle without it. However, I was stopped in my briefing by the sound of the bell.

Billy brought in Inspector George Mann, thankfully saving me the need to run through the details a second time.

"I am glad to have you with us," I told him, having renewed our brief acquaintance. "No doubt Watson will be along shortly. He was an excellent advocate on your behalf."

"Pleased to hear it," he said and settled down with Johnson and Wiggins to listen to my summary of the case.

"I can see why the doctor was playing his cards close to his chest," said Mann, once I had finished, "it certainly is a potentially inflammatory affair. If the details of this were to be leaked to the press…"

"Indeed." I couldn't help but laugh. "The last thing we need is the involvement of more reporters."

The joke seemed to pass above their heads, a not uncommon experience for me.

"There would be rioting in the streets," Johnson said. "People would go mad."

"I sometimes think very little encouragement is needed on that score," Mann said.

Wiggins nodded and gave a wry smile. "You're not wrong there. People like a ruckus and no mistake."

"We'll have enough of one by ourselves tonight," said Mann. "And I for one expect trouble from our guide as well as the man he's leading us to."

"You're quite right," I said, "and we all need to remember it. There is no doubting that, whatever happens, it benefits Kane were none of us to come out of those sewers alive."

"You think he intends to double-cross us?" asked Johnson.

"Most certainly," I replied. "I'd be exceptionally surprised if he didn't."

"All good fun," he replied, "and I'd better mind myself and all." He pulled a thick black stocking from his coat pocket. "On the slightest off-chance we do manage to survive the night, I'd better make sure the bugger don't recognise me." He pulled the stocking over his head. "My life wouldn't be worth thruppence if it got around that I'd been fraternising with you lot!"

I confess it often slipped my mind that Johnson took a terrible risk simply being seen with me. He truly was a man from another world.

Downstairs the bell rang. Given the length and stridency of the tone it could only be Challenger.

Billy answered it and the professor's voice echoed up the stairway like a sergeant major issuing the call to charge.

I checked the time. Kane would soon be here, but where was Watson?

That answer came soon enough when Billy entered alongside Challenger. "Telegram for you, Sir," he said, handing it over and stepping as far away from Challenger as he could. It was clear he was quite terrified of the man. I have noticed people are often intimidated by such physical giants, and I always think it strange. What do any of us have to fear from brute strength? That's what fire pokers and revolvers are for. It's a powerful brain that should scare us.

I opened the telegram. It read:

HOLMES I HAVE YOUR FRIEND [STOP] HE WILL BE HELD AS INSURANCE AGAINST YOUR BEHAVIOUR [STOP] DO NOT MAKE ME TURN HIM INTO SOMETHING HE WILL REGRET [STOP]

"Like a confirmed bachelor, perhaps?" I muttered.

"What's that, Holmes?" asked Challenger.

It was good that he addressed me by name as, given the volume of his inquiry, I might otherwise have assumed he was asking the question of Mr Goss, the gentleman who lived three doors down.

"It is our enemy playing his hand," I said and offered him the telegram to pass around the room.

"What are we going to do now?" Johnson asked. "Surely we can't call the hunt off?"

"Indeed not," I agreed. "That is precisely what we can't do."

CHAPTER THIRTY-FIVE

Kane didn't keep us long. It was nine o'clock precisely when the door bell rang and we once more heard Billy move to answer it.

"Now, Gentlemen," I said, "keep your eyes open and your wits sharp, our enemies are at our throats from this moment forth."

We listened to Kane's heavy feet on the stairs, Johnson making sure his disguise was safely in place. The door opened and, again, I was struck by the daunting stature of the creature that filled the doorframe.

"A party of adventurers indeed," he said, a harsh sniff emanating from beneath the heavy veil as he set his sensitive nose to work. "Might I be introduced? I like to know the names of gentlemen I am expected to blithely trust my life to."

He might brag of his intelligence but he could split an infinitive with the best of them.

"They might reasonably say the same thing," I replied, "to a man in a disguise as heavy and theatrical as yours."

"I hide nothing," he replied, stepping into the room and pulling away his hat and veil to reveal the dog's head beneath.

There was a drawing in of breath as they took him in. Precisely the effect he had hoped for of course.

I had described him accurately but words could not convey the monstrousness of Kane's appearance. I had discussed the resonance and timbre of his voice, even speculated how it must be produced considering the limited dog's palate, but to hear it was something else again. I told them precisely how many teeth he had, and their approximate length, but to see them glint in the lamplight was far more inspiring. Like good opera and a perfectly cooked chateaubriand steak, Kane was a thing to be experienced rather than discussed.

"Astounding!" Challenger said, stepping closer. "You, Sir, are a positive miracle. I have never seen the like."

"After tonight you never will again," Kane replied. "Kindly keep your distance! I am not a museum exhibit to be gawped at."

Challenger raised a bushy eyebrow. "I was hardly gawping, Sir. I am Professor George Edward Challenger, a foremost authority on… Well, almost anything you might choose to mention. So when you have my attention you might bear in mind it is the attention of the very best."

"Never heard of you," Kane replied. "But then I have very little time for experts. Their inability to agree the truth makes me want to chew their faces off." He looked to Johnson. "And what facial non-conformity are you trying to hide, eh? Given what you see before you, you must be a very ugly man indeed to stay so bashfully covered."

"I've had a few complaints in my time, it's true," Johnson said.

"But it's my anonymity rather than your comfort that I'm trying to preserve."

"We all have our secrets, Kane," I said. "And the better they are maintained, the less we need to worry about each other."

"But you already know all my secrets I think," said Kane.

"I doubt that," I told him. "I doubt that very much."

"I'm sure we have better things to do than stand here talking," Mann said. "Might I suggest we get on with them?"

"Quite so," I agreed. "I suggest you let us know the area we're heading in and I'll have Billy commandeer us a pair of cabs."

"King's Cross," Kane said. "We can walk from there."

"Very well," I replied, before calling to Billy.

Kane turned to Mann. "And who are you?" he asked. "You have the unwelcome smell of the constabulary to you. I made it clear to Mr Holmes that I didn't wish there to be any official law enforcement here this evening."

"Then he followed your wishes," Mann replied. "I'm a private agent, much like Wiggins here. Though I do most of my business in the country."

"Hmm…" Kane gave another loud sniff. "I can smell it on you – greenery and mud. I don't like it."

"Then I shan't make the mistake of inviting you to tea," Mann replied.

I stepped into Watson's room, helping myself to his revolver. If the night went as I hoped, I would be able to hand it to him in person.

Billy called up to us that he had secured transport. Cautiously, with Kane back beneath his veil, we made our way down onto the street.

CHAPTER THIRTY-SIX

I travelled with Kane in one cab while the rest followed on behind. I was unwilling to let him out of my sight and it gave the others a chance to converse more openly. In actuality this probably meant that they had to listen to Challenger talk at them. I wondered if I might be fortunate enough to discover that Johnson had been forced to throttle him before we reached our destination. It would certainly allow the rest of the evening to pass more peacefully. Sadly, this was not to be the case.

Once we arrived at King's Cross, Kane led us behind the station and into the warren of backstreets that huddle around the railway tracks.

Shortly, we descended to the track itself, walking carefully beside the rails. Every few minutes a train would pass, pistons hammering in a percussive, chaotic row.

"Mind yourselves," Kane said, as if we needed warning. "It gets darker along here where the cut deepens and the trains will rip you from your feet without their drivers even noticing. We are nothing but flies buzzing around an elephant's ear." He had a rather poetic turn of phrase when he turned his canine mind to it.

"I saw a man lose his arm once," Johnson said. "Had too much to drink hadn't 'e? Fell down next to the track, stuck his arms out to stop his face from hitting the ground. Boom!" He mimed a train sweeping past. "Bad timing and the 13.14 to Colchester had it off just below the shoulder. Didn't even slow down, probably had no idea it had happened. The bloke in question was a bit slow on the uptake himself, mind you, only noticed a problem when he shook his fists at the driver and found himself one short."

Wiggins laughed at that just as another train made its deafening way past.

After a few more minutes, Kane halted the party and pointed at a drainage cover in the ground.

"Our entrance," he announced, pulling a short crowbar from a pocket inside his coat.

"Allow me," said Challenger, taking the crowbar from him and flipping up the drain cover as if it weighed nothing. He handed the crowbar back to Kane, smiling. "It's not just my brain that's powerful," he said.

"No," Kane agreed. "Your personality is just as indomitable."

"Now then," said Wiggins, "let's try and keep this as friendly as possible, shall we? No doubt there's enough down there waiting to do us harm without our fighting amongst ourselves."

Kane didn't reply just gestured towards the uncovered hole. "After you."

Wiggins looked to the hole, and the top of the ladder just visible within it, and sighed. He glanced at me, looking for the confirmation to go ahead. Naturally I gave it.

Mann followed Wiggins, then Johnson, then Challenger – somewhat irritated at having to wait his turn. Finally there was only Kane and I left on the surface.

"I think you should go next," I said to Kane, "just so you can tell them which way we should be walking."

"Still don't trust me, eh?" Kane replied.

"Naturally not," I replied. "I'm not an idiot after all."

Kane offered that disturbing grin of his, a smile that spoke of animal hunger rather than humour. "We'll see about that," he replied, and began to climb down the ladder.

I descended after him.

CHAPTER THIRTY-SEVEN

Descending into the tunnel we were hit by the oppressive air, not just the reek of the sewer water that rushed by but also the heavy sense of age and damp. The world from above rarely made itself felt in these long chambers. Fresh air, the cool, clean scent of a winter's breeze, these were things that had never intruded down here. This was a world of waste and rot, Moreau's world.

"I've been in some unpleasant places in my time," said Challenger, "landscapes terrible and dangerous. I have choked on the sulphurous outpourings of an active volcano, the fetid aroma of freshly gutted buffalo, the assault on the nostrils that is Delhi at high summer. And yet this is undoubtedly the most foul smelling, and unappealing."

"We are not here to act as tourists," Kane said. "We are here for business."

"And dark business at that," agreed Wiggins.

"On the subject of which –" There was the scrape of a match and

Johnson lifted up an illuminated lantern "– We'll be needing a bit of extra light."

"If you can't manage without," Kane hissed. "Though I would have preferred not to present such an obvious target. They will see us coming from some distance away."

"Yeah, well, I can't see for a foot in front of my face without it," Johnson said. "So we'll have to manage, wont we?"

I could see Kane's point but thought it particularly ill-advised to stumble around in the dark. "We cannot manage without light for now," I said, "so we might as well accept the fact and get moving."

"Many expeditions are a matter of compromise," Challenger said as we began to work our way along the tunnel. "I remember, during a particularly arduous trek along the banks of the Amazon, I was forced to…"

"Must he talk all the time?" said Kane. "You can hear his bellowing for miles, I'm sure."

Of course, I agreed with Kane on this point, not that Challenger gave me time to admit as much.

"Right!" he shouted. "That's it! I have been more than tolerant of your disgraceful behaviour, you blasted mongrel!" He raised his fists. "We will not go a step further until I have pounded a little of the insolence out of you."

"Gentlemen!" I whispered. "Need I remind you that this is an occasion for stealth and discretion?"

"Discretion my sainted arse!" Challenger roared. "I want to box the ears of this dog-headed cur! This mangy upstart!"

Kane reached out and lashed at Challenger with one leather-mittened paw.

There was the click of a revolver being cocked and both Mann and Wiggins were pointing their guns at Kane.

"Calm down," said Mann, "before you jeopardise everything."

"That's the spirit!" Challenger said. "We'll show the arrogant pup where he stands."

"I was talking to you," Mann replied. "For a genius you're not awfully clever. Now shut up and let's get moving."

Whether Challenger was simply shocked into compliance or actually saw the logic of Mann's words was impossible to tell but, after a harrumph of indignation, he pushed past Kane and began to walk along the tunnel.

All of which served to prove to me why it is rarely worthwhile to work in company. Challenger was supposed to be a genius and yet, as far as I could see, his temper had replaced his brain to the point of rendering him a liability. How I wished for Watson and no other, at least with him by my side I knew I had someone on whom I could depend.

We had walked for only a few more minutes before Kane held up his hand for us to stop.

"Extinguish the lanterns," he said.

"We can't see without them," Johnson insisted.

"You will have to manage. We are close now and father's watchdogs will be on the prowl."

Johnson looked to me and I could see no choice but to accede to Kane's suggestion. I nodded and the lantern was extinguished.

The first few moments were severely disorientating as our other senses fought to compensate. The smell grew stronger, the sound of rushing water louder. Shuffling along that narrow footpath, it was an effort to keep moving, running my fingers along the brick wall to my right to keep a regular distance.

Soon other noises joined the rush of water and the sound of our footsteps. Some distance ahead I could hear something scraping along the bricks of the path. Was this one of the guard dogs Kane had warned us about? Could there be other animals living down here? There were rats of course, I had occasionally heard them call to one another in the dark. But the noise we heard now was certainly from something much bigger. The way it pulled itself along the path, it sounded like something limp, being dragged. Behind me I heard someone cock their revolver. Perhaps the creature heard it too because, all of a sudden, there was a high-pitched squeal and it came for us.

We still couldn't see it but the noise was easy to follow. It launched itself and bounced off the wall to our left. Then dragged itself, quite impossibly, across the ceiling.

Someone fired and in the flash of the muzzle we could glimpse a mass – amorphous, slick and possessing altogether too many limbs. It roared, and both Wiggins and Johnson aimed their revolvers. Four shots were fired in quick succession, rapid bursts of light like fireworks, the afterglow of which hung green and blue before our eyes as the creature howled once more, clearly hurt.

"Stop firing!" Kane shouted, as the creature lost its grip and hit the water. We were doused by the splash that resulted from the creature's fall. Blind, wet and panicked, we all held our backs against the wall, guns at the ready in case the creature came for us again.

"What the hell was that?" Wiggins asked. "Damned thing looked like an angry hot air balloon."

It was a grotesque description but an accurate one.

"Who knows where he gets all his creatures from?" said Kane. "By the time he's finished blending them together, it's all but impossible to tell what they were originally."

"How many more of these things can we expect?" I asked.

"As many as you like if they're as easy to kill," Johnson said.

"They won't be," Kane said.

"I will face as many of the beasts as fate chooses to offer," Challenger said. "I for one am absolutely fascinated by them!" He sighed. "If only I could examine the body of that one, who knows what we could learn from its cadaver?"

"As much as I sympathise with your hunger for information," I said, "this is not a scientific expedition. Perhaps once our mission is accomplished, there will be time for such things."

"I will make time," Challenger said.

"Might I suggest we keep moving?" Mann said. "After all we have certainly just announced our presence to anything in the vicinity."

"He's right," Kane added. "We certainly have no chance of attacking by surprise now. Those gunshots will have carried for miles down here."

"In that case," Johnson said, striking a match, "you won't mind if I have my lantern back. I'm not walking blind into whatever's up there waiting for us."

Kane growled but said nothing, no doubt he could tell that there was little point in arguing; Johnson meant to have his way and he would not be swayed.

We continued along the tunnel, Kane keeping several feet in front with Johnson lighting the way behind him.

It was not long before we would come face to face with the next "guard dog". In fact it had assuredly been heading towards us the minute it heard the first gunshot.

The first sign that it was nearby came from Challenger rather than Kane. "The water," he said. "Something is making its way towards us."

We stopped and listened. I was immediately aware of what Challenger had noticed. (No doubt I would have heard it earlier had I not been concentrating on what lay ahead.) "The splash of the water is getting louder. Something large is swimming its way towards us."

"I became extremely attuned to the sound of the water during my trips up the Amazon," Challenger said. "At night, enemy tribes would try to sneak up on us, canoeing slowly up the river. It got so that you listened for any change in the tempo and quality of the waves. Noticing something untoward could be the difference between life and death."

I could not help but be drawn into speculation with regards the nature of the creature that made its way towards us. What manner of thing would it be? Fish or fowl?

Even when it attacked it was hard to tell, there was a sudden rush of water and Johnson shouted, holding up his lantern in order to direct the light as clearly onto the beast as possible. It rose from the sewage as if elevated by wires. Whatever legs powered it up into the air, they were strong indeed.

It made no noise but a mouth that might well have belonged to a shark – a thin gash of scar tissue and tiny, glinting teeth – snapped at the air as it launched itself at Johnson.

He was quick to fire, but Johnson was not a shootist. His childhood had been one where disagreements were settled with fists and clubs. He had never had cause to develop the skill of drawing a clear aim under pressure. The shot went wide, perhaps it grazed the creature but it certainly didn't slow it down. It was almost on him as I took my own shot.

Now, of all my skills, shooting is the one I have practised the least. Mainly due to the anger of my landlady with regards the state of the walls afterwards. Nonetheless, when possessed of a clear mind and a focussed aim, I can be reassuringly formidable. My bullet went directly into the creature's head, a lumpen, disgusting thing that could have been part ox as much as shark. I wasn't the only one to fire – I felt two other bullets pass me. The impact of the rounds had little effect on the creature. It continued its progress towards Johnson even as he fired a second shot. This one, at closer range, hit it in its open mouth. There was a high-pitched whine and the creature landed on him, its mouth still snapping – a soft clapping of cartilaginous lips and a grinding of its rows of teeth. Johnson screamed, an unnerving sound to come from such a brute of a man.

"Hold your fire!" I shouted. There was no need to waste further ammunition, my shot had been perfect and must have destroyed the brute's brain. What was left was no more than its death throes, the last few vestiges of life before it gave up completely. Of course, in those last moments it could still do more than enough damage, as the scream from Johnson had attested.

"Get it off him!" Wiggins shouted, pushing past me and moving towards where the creature had fallen on his comrade. Kane beat him to it, grabbing the slimy beast by one of its limbs and tugging it back into the water where it fell with a splash.

"It has probably killed him," he said. "That scream had the sound of death to it."

"Trust you to wish me the best," came Johnson's voice, weak but steady. "It's taken a blasted chunk out of me but I'm not done for yet."

"Let me take a look," I said, picking up the fallen lantern and holding it over Johnson so as to examine his wounds. If Watson had been with us then I have no doubt that he would have been able to perform a more thorough investigation. Even with my limited knowledge I could see that Johnson would bleed to death unless we got a tourniquet on him. I told them as much.

"We haven't time for this!" Kane growled. "The rest of the creatures will be right behind him."

"All the more reason to work quickly then," I said. "We don't leave our wounded to die, certainly not when a few weeks and a regular change of dressing would see him back on his feet again." I like to think Watson would have been proud of my sensitivity.

"Simple as that?" Johnson asked. "Told you it weren't nothing, didn't I?"

"I have the very thing," said Challenger. He dropped to his knees, swung his backpack from his shoulder and began to hack at it with a knife. In a few moments he had removed one of the leather straps that bound it shut. "Is there space to cinch that above the wound?" he asked.

"Just about," I replied, running it around the top of his thigh and inside his crotch.

"Careful where you go strapping that, Mr Holmes," said Johnson. "I don't want to lose anything more precious than my leg." He gave a chuckle that turned into a moan as I pulled the leather strap through its buckle and fixed it as tightly as I could.

"He needs taking back to the surface," I said. "There's no use in his continuing with us. Wiggins can take him."

The young lad's face fell at the idea of his leaving us, but I could tell that his loyalty towards Johnson outweighed any argument.

"I could always come back," he suggested, "once I've stashed him somewhere safe."

I pulled him close and whispered in his ear, disguising the move with a hug. I trusted Kane didn't know me well enough to appreciate how distasteful I find that sort of thing.

My natural inclination is simply to write down what I said to him at that point but I know that Watson would never forgive me – he does so love to leave things out to increase dramatic effect during his climaxes. It seems childish and unnecessary to me, but I will accede to his tastes as this account is, by the lion's share, his.

I turned to Kane, curious to tell whether he had heard me. His face, however, was impossible to read.

"Let's keep moving," I said, pointing ahead and pushing past Kane so as to lead the way.

I gave one last glance at Wiggins, who winked at me. Then he lifted Johnson up and began to head back the way we had come.

CHAPTER THIRTY-EIGHT

So, our party was now two members down. It could have been worse – one of us could have been dead.

I was sure that, by leading the way, I might limit any future accidents. After all, bar Kane, I was the one who had some idea of what we were walking towards.

"We are nearly there," he said, that growl of a voice coming from just behind me. "There is a hole in the tunnel wall just around the next bend. It used to be part of a factory I think – huge storage areas and chambers, abandoned until we came."

"We came?" I asked. "I thought you were born down here?"

There was a slight pause. "Indeed, it was just a turn of phrase."

He was growing less cautious now we were nearly there. I took that as a good sign. After all, it would be easier all round if we could just drop the pretence.

We turned the corner and Kane pushed past me. "I will lead," he said. "It is difficult to find if you don't know where it is."

We gathered at the entrance, the hole covered by a draped length of sacking. "We are here," said Kane. "We should enter quietly, my father may have left someone on guard. If we can sneak up on them quietly we stand a fair chance."

"Quietly?" asked Mann. "It's been as noisy as the Boer War down here so far."

Kane simply stared at him so I took it upon myself to take control.

"We will do as Kane says," I told them. "Whatever happens, stay calm."

The time had come. I suspected I knew what would lie on the other side of that wall. I was fairly certain that I had the measure of how events would play out once we stepped into Mitchell's lair. Now I would find out if I had been right.

One by one, we stepped beyond the sacking, entering the pitch-darkness of the room beyond. There was a smell, that sweet animal scent of the zoo. From the way the sound of our footsteps echoed I could tell the room we were entering was of a reasonable size. I knew as much when there was the sound of a struck match and the beam of a lantern shone upon us. Then another, and another, and yet one more...

We were surrounded by the beast men, holding up their lanterns and looking at us with their animal eyes.

"Ah, Holmes," said Mitchell, still wearing his foul pig's-head mask, "so good of you to join us."

Kane went to stand by his master's side.

"You really should have stayed within the safe walls of Baker Street," Mitchell continued, his voice distorted as it echoed around the inside of that swinish cowl. "Now that you are all here I can do whatever I wish with you, my experiments can recommence with fresh supplies! You are entirely at my mercy!"

All of which, naturally came as something of a relief.

PART SIX

THE ARMY OF DR MOREAU

WATSON

I don't think I have ever been so disturbed as during those few hours after my capture. Through my association with Holmes I have found myself in perilous situations many times. I have been chased by a wild dog on Dartmoor, shot at by vengeful big game hunters with air rifles, threatened by Thuggee occultists and even injected by Elwood Dunfires, the notorious Babel Poisoner. For all that, I was never more aware of the fragility of my own existence than when faced with the singular madness of Albert Mitchell!

He talked at some length as we travelled in his coach, listing mankind's crimes against nature with the fervency and imbalance that can only come from the truly lunatic.

"Moreau wished to create a new species in that lab we shared," he explained, many, *many* times over, "and he succeeded, through me! Watching the acts of atrocity he committed on those poor animals, the heartless cruelties, the pointless agony…"

"Didn't stop him though, did you?" I could hardly help but point out after I had heard the story several times. "I agree fully with your attitude towards vivisection – I have yet to see a worthwhile justification for it. I, however, would simply have punched the blackguard on the jaw and let the animals go." I stared out of the window at the passing street, rather that than look into his mad eyes. "But then, I've always been a rather practical man."

"You do not know," he roared, "could never understand what it was like!"

"Yes, yes –" I admit I tried to placate him. It would help nobody were I to end up dead before we even reached our destination "– I dare say that's the case."

He stared at me, face red, spittle on his chin. He had been the very model of urbanity last time I had seen him. It would seem that now, having embraced his plan wholeheartedly, the few human traits he possessed were fading fast. His hands clutched at the legs of his trousers, tugging at the material; his feet rolled on the floor, heel to toe, as if he were impatient to run. He reminded me of a caged animal, preparing to bolt the minute he could see open air.

"What have you done with the Prime Minister?" I asked, hoping that a change of subject might help to calm him down.

"Lord Newman will become one of my greatest supporters," he replied. "After all, we share so many of the same concerns."

I did not relish the sound of that. "What have you done to him?" I asked again.

He smiled, once more the alpha male. "You will see soon enough. He is a greater man than he ever was."

We arrived outside what appeared to be an abandoned warehouse. As far as I could tell we were somewhere in the area of King's Cross. I considered making a run for it the minute the door was opened, but one look at the eyes of our feline driver changed my mind. I knew that my chances of getting out alive would drop dramatically once we were inside the building, but if this brute lived up to his natural heritage he would be fast as well as strong. There was no chance I'd be able to outrun him.

I was grabbed by the shoulder, and I could feel thick claws pierce the material of my jacket. If I pulled away he meant to make sure I left a piece of me behind!

"I can't promise you will be comfortable," Mitchell said. "But I doubt you'll have to endure my company for long."

"Well that's a relief."

He stared at me, seemingly at a loss as to why I was being so rude. That's the problem with lunatics – they're not awfully self-aware.

"I had hoped that you might be able to assist me," he said. "As a medical man you would have been an extremely beneficial companion."

"As a medical man I couldn't lift a scalpel to help you."

"You say that now, but let us see if you can maintain that dismissive attitude once you see what I have achieved."

I was led inside the building, and my first impression was of the foul stench that clung to its ancient brick walls. I remember during my time in Afghanistan entering a barn that had been used to house a herd of goats. The sun had baked the inside of that barn, making the air hot and fetid, and filled with the aromas of hair, food and waste. I had been forced to run for the open before the atmosphere caused me to vomit.

This building was much larger, of course, and therefore the smell was not so strong. Still, I couldn't help but think back to that Afghan hut.

The floor was filthy, littered with torn bedding, half-chewed bones and dark stains I didn't wish to guess at. For all Mitchell's talk of civilisation, it was clear his animal army hadn't stepped far from their feral behaviour.

Mitchell clearly sensed my disgust. No doubt it showed clearly on my face.

"I am not here to strip away what makes our animal friends what they are," he explained, "unlike Moreau with his determination that they should be made vegetarian, stripped clean of their urges and needs."

"Fear the Law –" I said "– Isn't that what you shouted when you wanted them to behave? Doesn't sound like real freedom to me."

"Well," Mitchell squirmed slightly, "I'll admit I have had to maintain some sense of order, just to ensure we're all working towards the same goal. It's in their best interests."

"That's what all dictators say."

He led me down several flights of stairs then through to a small side room, the central feature of which was a large column covered with a heavy black sheet.

"Here," he said, "then you will finally understand the miracles I have created."

He tugged at the sheet, revealing a tall glass water tank. Inside, floating, fully clothed, was Lord Newman, the Prime Minister.

"Dear God, man!" I shouted, circling the tank to try to find a method of opening it. "He'll drown!"

"If he were going to drown," Mitchell replied, "he would have done so long ago." He pulled his fob watch from his waistcoat and checked the time. "Our noble guest has been in there for nearly an hour."

"Impossible."

"See for yourself, he still lives."

I pressed my face up against the glass, looking the dignitary in the eyes. His long hair and beard, so often criticised by the opposition as undignified, looked decidedly so now, bobbing around his pale face like seaweed fronds. His thin lips were tightly pressed together, as if he were holding his breath, and yet his skin showed none of the ruddy tones one would expect from a man deprived of oxygen. As I looked, his hair parted and just for a moment I glimpsed the organs that had newly grown on either side of his throat – narrow, fleshy slits that rippled as they allowed air bubbles to filter between them.

"Dear God!" I exclaimed. "You've given him gills!"

"Only indirectly. I injected him with the serum I have prepared, that Holy Grail of governmental research. He has simply adapted to his environment the quickest and simplest way his body could think of."

"But that's…" I couldn't finish my sentence. I was simply too in awe of the sight in front of me – the absurd, grotesque impossibility of it.

Suddenly Lord Newman convulsed, his whole body twitching like a fish caught on a line.

"Damn," said Mitchell, stepping closer to the glass. "I was so sure he would last longer than the rest."

"Longer than… What are you talking about man? What's happening to him?"

He convulsed again and a shocking gobbet of blood burst from between those tightly pressed lips. It hung in the water for a moment, then sunk, immediately followed by another, and then one more. Soon his whole body was thrashing, and the water grew increasingly pink as he haemorrhaged.

"Every time," said Mitchell, "the body goes so far and then breaks down."

"You've got to get him out of there!" I shouted, looking around for something I could use to break the glass. I moved no more than a couple of feet before the leopard creature gripped me by the arms and raised me slightly off the floor. I thrashed in his grip, just as Lord Newman thrashed in the tank, neither of us to any positive effect.

"There's no point," said Mitchell, staring through the glass as Lord Newman slowly vanished in the murky soup. "He'll be dead in a few moments. It's almost akin to tissue rejection, as if the whole body begins to reject itself once the changes bed in. Fascinating –" he looked away "– but so terribly disappointing. He was to be my spokesman for the brave new age. Mind you," he grinned, "I didn't vote for him, did you?"

"Inhuman bastard!" I was beside myself with rage, not caring that the claws of the creature were tearing holes in my upper arms.

"Oh yes," said Mitchell, "isn't that the point?" He looked once more at the water in the tank, still and red now, and the hirsute silhouette that floated within. "Shame. Still, if at first you don't succeed…" He looked at me, and the ferociousness of his lunacy burned hot in those eyes. "Let's hope you manage to last a little longer, eh?"

I was carried out, and dragged down the adjoining corridor to another small room.

Mitchell pulled a bunch of keys from his pocket and unlocked the door. "You'll have to forgive the smell," he said. "This is the secure area where we keep our animal friends when they first come into our care. They are understandably disorientated at first, and sore from their surgeries. We find it best to keep them somewhere dark and peaceful until they have come to their senses."

He opened the door and once more I was hit with my memories of that Afghan barn, before I was thrown inside and the darkness consumed me.

I landed painfully on my knees, and rolled to my side in what felt like damp straw.

My arms burned from where the creature's claws had drawn blood.

At that moment I could have happily killed Mitchell – he seemed to be the most terrible, loathsome beast of all.

Eventually I began to calm down, though the image of Lord Newman's death lingered with me in the darkness. I was simply unable to see anything else.

After a while, as much as I tried to nurture my moral indignation, my thoughts turned instead to my own predicament. Clearly I was to share the same fate as the Prime Minister. Perhaps not the water tank – I had a feeling that Mitchell would always be eager to experiment afresh – but certainly something like it. Perhaps I would be buried alive, left to writhe like a worm until I ruptured into the soil. Or would I be dissected – forced to regrow myself ad nauseam like a lizard that has shed its tail?

I have often had cause to imagine death. Indeed, in the months since Mary's passing I almost wished it on myself. But not like this. I could never have imagined anything approaching the horror of a death like this.

Still, as the hours went by, I could see no other way out of it. All I could hope for was that an opportunity to break free might present itself. Certainly, I would rather die at the hands of one of my animal pursuers, cut down as I made a break for the open, than become a scientific horror of the kind I had witnessed.

And then the moment came. I heard footsteps advancing on the door to the room, the sound of the key in the lock.

"It's now or never," I said. "Get ready John, old man!"

But Mitchell had not come for me. Instead he had brought me company.

"Go on!" he shouted and, just for a moment in the light thrown from the open doorway, I saw Holmes, Challenger and Mann stumble into the room. Then the door was shut and all was dark once more.

"Holmes?" I shouted. "I might have hoped to see you on better terms."

"Ah!" my friend's voice replied. "Is that you Watson? Not the most convivial of surroundings is it?"

"Damned disgrace," Challenger shouted. "Treated like a blasted animal!"

"If only his intentions were that kind," I said.

"Yes," Mann agreed, "I have a feeling we'll know worse yet."

So, this is where my insistence on having the inspector join us had led. His wife would likely never set eyes on him again, poor man. *So much for your principles, you old fool*, I thought.

"It's not good," I said, before telling them of the fate of Lord Newman.

"Unbelievable," said Mann.

"Just what I said, myself," I admitted. "But I can't really see a way out of our situation. He has an army of those beasts to fight against. We're outnumbered, overpowered and trapped here in the dark."

"I know," said Holmes, and I could swear that the man was smiling. "I've got him just where I want him!"

Which is when the room shook in response to a nearby explosion.

CARRUTHERS

"Mr Carruthers," Holmes said, "the role you play will be of vital importance, rest assured of that."

I can't deny that was music to this old boy's ears. If there's one thing we Carruthers relish, it's pitching our all against the odds. Whether it be hanging off a glacier in Asia, facing down a tiger in India or surrounded by the beady eyes of crocodiles in South America, Roger Carruthers has always taken a singular pleasure in staring death in the face and cocking his not inconsiderable snook at the beggar.

Once Watson had left, Holmes explained his plan.

"There is no doubt in my mind that Kane means to lead us into a trap but I see no better alternative than letting that trap be sprung in the hope that it leads us to our quarry.

"What we need is someone with sufficient tracking experience to follow our trail at a safe distance. Kane is no fool and he would certainly be aware of a large party at our heels. He may also have accomplices set out to ensure we are not followed."

I nodded, agreeing with his supposition. "All of which it will be my job to avoid, follow you anyway and then bring the reinforcements?"

"Exactly."

"And I suppose it's my job to provide the reinforcements?" Mycroft asked.

"Naturally," said Holmes.

So it was, that at nine o'clock both myself and Mycroft Holmes found ourselves dressed from head to toe in coachman's coats, standing to one end of Baker Street.

"Exciting, what?" I said.

Mr Holmes couldn't quite match my enthusiasm. "It's cold and horrid. I make it a point of principle not to leave my armchair after ten o'clock."

"Then you have an hour to go!"

"Ten o'clock in the morning. Movement is overrated, give me warm fires and a willing waiter over all this tiresome gadding about."

"Gadding about? You've barely covered a mile. I dread to think what you would make of some of my expeditions."

"Expeditions are ridiculous," he agreed. "Find somewhere you like and then stay there. I can only assume there is something deeply wrong with a man who hasn't the decency to settle. What's wrong with you? Were you bitten by a comfortable cushion as a child?"

I couldn't help but laugh, though Mycroft, as dry as a Quaker, merely raised a bushy, white eyebrow.

"Here he comes," I said, nodding towards the large silhouette that was advancing on the front step of 221b. "Big feller, isn't he?"

Kane rang the bell and was shortly admitted. "Time to present ourselves as gentlemen of worthy employment," I said, putting on my hat, picking up my whip and climbing into the driver's seat of one of the cabs Mycroft had arranged.

"Such an embarrassment," Mycroft said, doing the same. "I promised faithfully to Mother I'd do no such thing."

His cab gave an audible creak as he clambered into position and we watched for sign of Holmes' page boy. We didn't have to wait long. The young lad was soon waving at us from the front step.

"And off we go!" I gave the horses a nudge and we made our way along the street.

I must admit I was somewhat concerned as to whether I would manage behind the reins, but the pair of horses Mycroft had found were the very epitome of good behaviour. It was therefore with some modicum of professionalism that I took both Holmes and Kane onboard my cab and headed off in the direction of King's Cross.

I tapped the brim of my hat to Mycroft's chap, Fellowes, as we passed him and his small party of security officers. They were well hidden aboard what appeared to be a dray cart, and would surely be on our tail once we were a short distance ahead.

I did my best to eavesdrop on the conversation going on behind me, but they talked so quietly that I could barely grasp a word above the sound of the horses' hooves.

Eventually we arrived at the station. I heard Mycroft approach behind me, and all our passengers disembarked.

I was under no illusion that this would be their final destination. Kane would work harder than that to disguise his master's location.

Still, we had made the first stage painlessly enough. I took the payment from Holmes with a suitably gracious smile and made a show of pulling away from the station and leaving them to it. I stopped outside the station exit, appearing for all the world like a cabbie waiting for his next fare. In fact, Mycroft had just such a problem, having to awkwardly discourage a potential client by insisting that he was heading home to his bed. He obviously sounded convincing enough – the fact he would like to do nothing more probably helped – and he pulled away to meet with Fellowes.

Once I was sure that Holmes' party had cleared the area, I hopped down from my cab, threw my coat and hat in the back and replaced them with a dark worsted jacket and a small pack. I needed to move lightly but also be prepared – I was heading into dangerous territory.

Checking to see that Mycroft had rendezvoused with his men, I made to follow Holmes.

It was vitally important that I keep my distance without losing sight of them, a difficult task in a city, most especially when one has to forego the usual bushcraft tracking. There was precious little in the way of compressed undergrowth or damp, imprinted earth here. Not that I hadn't managed worse – you try and track a Sudanese native across the desert on a moonless night. See how sick you get of the taste of sand.

Once they had descended to walk along the rail tracks, my job was made considerably easier and I was able to hang back even further.

Holmes and I had agreed that they were unlikely to post anyone on watch until the actual tunnel entrance, though I had kept the old eyes peeled just in case. The moon was near full and my eyesight has long been used to working in low light.

I heard the sound of a manhole cover being lifted and cast aside.

There was precious little camouflage along that cutting, so I made the best use of the shadow, and drew close enough to have the party in sight as they descended underground.

While I waited I looked around, trying to decide where Kane would have left an accomplice. The most obvious vantage point was a signal box some short way past the tunnel entrance. Willing to wager on it being the chosen lookout point, I pressed myself into the undergrowth and worked my way behind it.

Peering through the dirty glass I could see a vague shape standing in the darkness and drew myself to the door as quietly as my years of hostile environments have taught me.

I was lucky in that the feller had his back to the doorway, eyes fixed intently on the tunnel entrance.

Accepting that one simply cannot march through the streets of London carrying a rifle, I had left the Remington at the hotel. I was nonetheless unwilling to go entirely unarmed. Mycroft had provided me with a Webley revolver, the butt of which I brought down with some force on the back of the lookout's head. A somewhat unsporting move on my part and it didn't sit easily with me. Still, one must sometimes forego morals in pursuit of the greater good.

I lit a match and glanced down into the face of a bizarre creature indeed. It had the short, snub beak of an eagle, its tiny black eyes no doubt perfect for observing in the darkness. It groaned as I rolled it over. Unwilling to kill unless absolutely necessary, I reached into my pack for some rope and bound and gagged the beast to the best of my ability.

Fairly sure that the coast would now be clear, I exited the signal box and made my way over to the tunnel entrance.

The manhole cover had been pulled partially back into place. I placed my ear to the slim gap and listened. They had moved some distance away.

I reached for my pack once more and set a match to the small lantern I had been carrying. Leaving it just to one side of the manhole, I descended a few steps down the ladder inside and listened once more. I could hear the faintest sounds of movement coming from my right.

Rising back up to the open air, I made a note of the direction I was walking in, folded it and placed it under the lantern. The breadcrumb trail had begun!

Back down in the tunnel, I waited a moment for the afterglow of the lantern to fade from my eyes. It would take them a few minutes to adjust, I knew, but if I used the wall to guide me then I should be able to draw close enough to Holmes and his party to keep them within earshot.

I must say that, despite the frankly awful smell, I found it intensely peaceful in those tunnels. There is something wonderful about having one's senses deprived, relying on the hypersensitivity of others. I almost seemed to float along in the darkness, caring not in the least that I couldn't see a thing in front of me, knowing simply that I was walking in the right direction and that I could no more get lost than water rolling down a drainage pipe.

I relished the fact that they were making more than enough noise to cover my pursuit. However sensitive Kane's ears might have been, there was no way he could have heard me over the sound of Challenger's frequent outbursts.

Then the first round of shooting began.

I kept my Webley in my hand and waited, listening intently for every clue as to what was happening. Holmes and I had agreed that there was little I could do in this situation. The important thing was to remain hidden until Mitchell's lair had been exposed. Once that was known (and the information passed on) then I was free to act as I liked but, until then, I was to reveal myself for no reason other than to protect my own life.

I heard the attacking creature splash into the water and the sound of excited chatter. Certainly the majority of them had prevailed then, I reasoned, and I continued to follow at a safe distance. At some point I must have passed the dead body of the creature that had attacked them, but in the darkness I had no way of knowing.

The next attack came shortly after and followed the same pattern – a volley of shots, the sound of the creature expiring into the water followed by enough chatter to let me know that at least some of the party had survived.

But then my ears picked up the sound of someone heading back in my direction.

I halted and, once again, kept my Webley ready. The last thing I wanted to do was use it. That would expose my presence all too effectively. But if they came upon me anyway, I would have little to lose.

They were carrying the lantern and it was only a few more moments before I recognised them as a friendly pair of faces.

"You must be Carruthers," the younger of the two whispered, as faintly as he could. "Holmes told me you were back here. My name's Wiggins and this 'ere waste of space is Shinwell Johnson."

"Pleased to meet you both," I said.

"Apparently we're nearly there," said Johnson. "Just a few more feet, according to Dog-Breath."

"Then might I suggest you gather Mycroft and his chaps?" I said. "I'll keep on Holmes' trail for now in case I can be of any assistance, but the sooner we have the weight of numbers the better."

"Righto."

I worked my way past them and continued after what remained of their party.

Again, I was unable to see the beast they had killed, though I could certainly smell it, even over the effluent. It had a distinct hint of the ocean to it, like a fishmonger's in high summer.

Not long after I had passed it, I heard the sound of shouting ahead and a light appeared from behind an ill-fitting curtain that hung on the wall.

Moving as close to it as I dared I could hear the sound of a man's voice.

"You really should have stayed within the safe walls of Baker Street," it said. "Now that you are all here I can do whatever I wish with you. My experiments can recommence with fresh supplies! You are entirely at my mercy!"

What a melodramatic old sock, I thought.

There were obviously a number of creatures on the other side of the curtain, and I waited to hear them file away before I pulled the fabric to one side and stepped through the ragged opening in the bricks.

I immediately felt something grab me and I turned with all the speed I could muster, bringing the revolver up and into the face of whatever had set its paws on me. It gave a short grunt but I wrapped my arms around its head, determined to muffle the noise, and swiftly wrenched its neck to one side. There was an awful crunching noise and the beast went limp in my arms.

The rest of the party had taken their light with them so I'll never know what manner of beast I slipped past the curtain and into the water beyond. It had lank, greasy hair and chunky teeth but I could tell no more.

I could hear the sound of the melodramatic Mitchell, no doubt holding forth on quite how brilliant he was. I chose not to listen, rather hung back and started to ferret in my pack for the dynamite.

Holmes and I had agreed that in all likelihood a distraction would be needed; I can think of little more distracting than a whopping great explosion so set about arranging one.

It nearly happened early when young Wiggins snuck up behind me and put his hand on my shoulder.

"Sorry," he said. "Johnson insisted he could manage so the stubborn oaf's off to fetch Mycroft. I thought you might need a hand."

"Considering I almost blew one of mine off when you made me jump," I admitted, "I'm only too glad of the offer. Keep an eye on that lot while I finish setting these fuses."

The building had clearly once been used for storage. Room after room of open space now filled with the detritus of those that had made their home here. Conscious of not causing enough destruction to either bring the whole lot down on our heads or block Mycroft's arrival with reinforcements, I ran a length of fuse from room to room, setting up a network of small explosions that I hoped would cause the requisite chaos when the time was right.

"He's locked them up," said Wiggins. "Get a move on, 'cause they'll be heading back this way any minute."

"Ready when you are, old chap," I told him. "Might I suggest you duck?"

At which point I lit the first fuse.

JOHNSON

Only went and got myself bitten by a bloody sharktopus, didn't I? I mean, seriously, the bloody thing went for me like a cross between a Chinese dinner and my mother-in-law. Would be me, wouldn't it? Not Rover or Professor Gob, nah… "Shinwell Johnson, have a bit of that! What's that, piece of your leg missing? Oh, yeah, that will have been me."

I shot it, of course, right in its pie-hole. Only it didn't think the bullet was filling enough, obviously, as it were still hungry. I knew a woman like that once, never met something wrapped in pastry she didn't like. Big girl. We used to call 'er… well, never mind what we used to call 'er, it's not a turn of phrase you're likely familiar with, though you've obviously had a pie in your time too if you don't mind me saying. No offence. You're a big lad though, like your school dinners.

Anyway, so it's bearing down on me and I shoot it right between the gnashers. I'd have aimed for somewhere more painful but, my eyes, I couldn't see nothing but mouth and teeth.

I reckon it were dead by the time it took a piece out of me, probably didn't get to do much more than swallow. Still, not much consolation to me is it? A bit to the right and it would have had more of a mouthful and I'd have been *Sheila* Johnson for the rest of me natural.

What's that? Where are they? Oh yeah... I was getting to that. Down there, turn right, keep going until you hear the sound of screaming. Hole in the wall ain't there?

Better get a bloody move on and all! You haven't got time to be hanging around here gassing all night 'ave you?

HOLMES

"You really should have stayed within the safe walls of Baker Street," Mitchell continued, his voice distorted as it echoed around the inside of that swinish cowl. "Now that you are all here I can do whatever I wish with you. My experiments can recommence with fresh supplies! You are entirely at my mercy!"

All of which, naturally, came as something of a relief.

Of course if I had been in Mitchell's shoes I would have had Kane lead us somewhere utterly unrelated, take us on a wild goose chase and then unleash the wild monsters on us. That way, in case something went wrong – and he was dealing with me so of *course* something might go wrong – you haven't just led your enemy right up to your front door. All in all, such an action might be most charitably described as moronic. But then you don't expect genius when you're talking to a man who wears a pig's head as a hat. People like that are simply not the brightest sparks.

"Remember," I told the rest of my party, "stay calm."

The last thing we needed was one of them to bolt and set the animals into a frenzy. And what creatures they were! The equine creation mentioned by Fellowes, the leopard, a ram with ancient curled horns, a vulpine fellow, whose long white hair suggested to me *Canis lupus arctos* (my collection does in fact contain all canine species, not simply the domestic dog. Not so ridiculous now, is it?).

"Calm?" asked Mitchell. "What have you got to be calm about? You have been an idiot, led straight here by the nose, a mindless oaf who scarcely warrants his reputation."

Well, I wasn't going to stand for that.

"Mindless oaf? Surely not. There has been little opportunity to exercise my brain on this particular case, I grant you, but that can hardly be taken as evidence of stupidity.

"Though I grant you I should have seen the pattern days ago. A greyhound trainer and a Parisian furrier go missing then Andre Le Croix, the chef perhaps most famous for his foie gras, the recipe for which proudly reads like a torture menu for the unfortunate animal that goes into making it." Watson thinks I pay no attention at all, this is far from true. I listen, I just do not always *care*. "Someone was clearly targeting people known for their mistreatment of animals. I presume it was Le Croix who ended up in a sack on the floor of the Bouquet of Lilies?"

Mitchell was clearly somewhat thrown by this sudden change in tempo, an effect I always find endlessly pleasurable. "That was all that was left of him by the time my friends here had dined on him."

"Poetic I'm sure, I suppose we should be thankful you didn't try to skin the furrier but merely settled for chaining him up and torturing him for a while."

"We let him off lightly."

"Oh shut up!" I shouted. I don't anger often but this fool, this second-rate scientist with his hand-me-down philosophies and theories, was really beginning to get my dander up.

"So much for keeping calm," I heard Inspector Mann mutter. I suppose he had a point.

"You are a charlatan!" I told Mitchell. "You claim to be fighting on the side of animals and yet you commit the most unspeakable acts upon them."

"I improve them!" he screamed. "I fulfil their potential."

"Really?" I looked to Kane. "What it must be to be so fulfilled."

He growled and stepped in front of his master, his "father", still as loyal as ever, whatever he might have told Watson and I.

"I am the equal of you," he insisted, drool forming around his jaw.

"Hardly, though we might have a similar skill for fetching sticks, I'll grant you that."

I reached into my pocket for the whistle I had purloined off Perry but he had been thinking the same thing. He grabbed my wrist, pulled my hand out of the pocket and took the whistle himself. He dropped it to the floor and stamped on it.

"We'll have no more of that," he said.

"I suppose to have fallen foul of it a third time would have been rather embarrassing," I said, only too aware that even if I could have incapacitated Kane the rest of the beasts would have remained fighting-fit. "It doesn't bode well for your little sideline does it, really?" I looked to Mitchell. "I presume his criminal activities have been helping to fund your hobby? Just think what you could have achieved with an intelligent crook at your disposal, no doubt by now you would have managed to build an actual army rather than just skulking in the sewers with a handful of mongrels. Like an impoverished farmer with a grudge."

"Holmes," said Challenger. "Not that I disagree old chap but you might want to mind your tongue."

"Wise advice," said Mitchell, "or one of my friends will bite it off."

"Very well," I replied, "let's get on with whatever lunatic plan you have in mind. Taking over the country? Killing all the no-tails? Installing scratching posts on all street corners?"

Mitchell clenched his piggy little fists but just about managed to stay in control. Unfortunately. It was probably extremely foolish of me but I was intrigued to see him reduced to his animal state.

"Lock them up with their friend," he said. "We'll see them on the operating table soon enough."

"Only a fool would operate on Professor Challenger!" bawled the man himself. "It would be like repainting Ming china."

"Come along, Professor," I told him. "There's time yet to impress your genius upon them."

We were led through the warehouse and I paid special attention to my surroundings, noting Mitchell's equipment and how many creatures we had to contend with. On the latter point, things were not far from my desultory comment to Mitchell. For all his grand talk, he was little more than a crackpot with dangerous pets. Once Mycroft arrived, we'd certainly have no problem in handling them.

We passed his surgery and I slowed my pace in order to take in as much detail as I could. The rest of the warehouse had been – much like Mitchell's brain – little more than empty chambers littered with animal faeces – this was a hive of order and efficiency.

"You admire my laboratory, Mr Holmes?" he asked, noticing my attention.

"It is at least lacking in bones and straw compared to the rest of your home from home," I replied and took the opportunity to walk in and have a quick look around.

"Come away from there!" he shouted. "You'll see it soon enough when you're underneath my knife!"

I stepped out and he made a considerable show of locking the door behind me. I continued along the passageway to the room that was to be our gaol cell.

Mitchell unlocked the door, threw it open and shouted at us to enter.

We did so with no more complaint.

"Holmes?" said the welcome voice of my Watson. "I might have hoped to see you on better terms."

"Ah!" I replied. "Is that you, Watson? Not the most convivial of surroundings is it?"

"Damned disgrace," Challenger shouted. "Treated like a blasted animal!"

"If only his intentions were that kind," said Watson.

He proceeded to tell us of the fate of Lord Newman, a further depressing note to the case. Not only had it descended into nothing more interesting than the hunt for a lunatic, that lunatic had already managed to kill his most distinguished captive. Well, second most distinguished.

"I can't really see a way out of our situation," continued the ever-fretful Watson. "He has an army of those beasts to fight against, we're outnumbered, overpowered and trapped here in the dark."

"I know," I told him, with a smile that he could not hope to see in the darkness. "I've got him just where I want him!"

Which is when Carruthers started blowing the place up, providing a most exemplary distraction.

"I don't suppose anyone has anything long and thin I might use to pick the lock?" I asked.

"Pick the lock," shouted Challenger. "What for?"

There was a resounding crack and the door swung open. I walked out, glancing at the imprint of his size fourteen boot on the paintwork. "You've been in Peru recently I perceive," I mentioned, noting the highly unusual colour of the clay deposit he left an inch to the right of the lock.

"Indeed," he replied, "it was much nicer than this damnable place."

"Then let us take our leave."

INSPECTOR MANN

Walking back out into the warehouse was an assault on our senses. The explosions continued and the animals were in a wild panic, screaming and howling as they ran to and fro trying to escape the loud noise and hails of brick.

"My first London investigation," I said, "and I'll be blown up before I see the end of it."

"Sorry to have dragged you into this," said Watson, over-thinking things as usual.

"Don't worry," I told him, "at least it will save me having to do the paperwork."

"What have you done?" Mitchell was screaming. "What have you done?"

He ran to the laboratory, Holmes and I hard on his heels.

There was a roar from the end of the corridor and Kane stood there, his mouth wide open as he growled his animal hatred at us.

"Gun!" shouted Watson. Holmes, not even breaking his stride, threw his revolver to him and darted into the laboratory after Mitchell.

"Stand down!" Watson shouted, pointing the gun at Kane. "Or I'll drop you where you stand."

Suddenly the wall to his left cracked as another explosion took its effect. He fell to his right, the gun tumbling from his hands.

"Watson!" Leaving Holmes, I ran to help him but the explosions had taken their toll on the structure of the old warehouse and the crack in the wall was only the beginning. With a soft crunch, the ceiling sagged and before I could get to the fallen doctor, there was a hail of bricks and plaster as the lot came caving in before me. "Watson!"

"He's a goner, man," said Challenger behind me. "If the bricks didn't get him, that damned dog soon will."

The passageway was impassable, we were sealed in and Watson was sealed out.

HOLMES

Mitchell ran straight towards his laboratory and I could only assume he had something in there he considered potent enough to help him regain the upper hand. I therefore felt it best to follow.

He struggled with the keys as the explosions rang out throughout the warehouse, but wrestled the door open and dashed inside.

I noticed Kane appear at the end of the hallway. I really didn't have the enthusiasm to be able to deal with both of them. Isn't it precisely for situations like this that you come in company?

"Gun!" Watson shouted and I took great pleasure in throwing it to him as I continued in my pursuit of Mitchell. Behind me I was aware of the collapse of part of the ceiling and wall, hardly surprising given the age of the building. I'd placed the majority of it at close to a hundred-and-twenty years old, though some of the bricks had dated from as far back as 1763. Given the temperature of the last few winters and the fact that the place had not been looked after for some years, it must have been fragile indeed. I wasn't aware that part of it had fallen on Watson.

After all, I can hardly be expected to notice *everything*.

"Come now, Mitchell," I said, stepping into the doorway of his laboratory. "There's no earthly use in running, we have reinforcements on the way."

"Who says I'm running?" he replied, grabbing a hypodermic syringe.

"This is a concentrated dose of my serum," he explained, rolling up his sleeve, "a chemical capable of turning me into a creature far more powerful than the rest of your pathetic species."

"Up until it kills you," I reminded him.

"Not me," he insisted, plunging the needle into his arm, "I'm too strong, I will develop! I will evolve!" He began to swell, his skin reddening. It was almost as if his madness was taking on physical shape, turning him into a flesh and bone illustration of his own anger and violence. The pig cowl stretched and distorted as his head continue to expand beneath it. The veins were rising on his forearms, blue lines as thick and jumbled as a map of the Underground trains.

"Evolve!!!" it shouted, the voice even more slurred than normal.

I glanced at the door and noticed he had left the keys in the lock. Evolution will never be a replacement for intelligence.

"Evolve your way out of a locked room then," I suggested, stepping outside and locking the door behind me.

He immediately began pounding on it as I walked away but to no avail; it was a stout door. I joined Mann and Challenger in front of the pile of bricks and mortar that had once been the floor above.

"Watson was caught in it," said Challenger. "I'm sorry."

"Don't be," I replied, filling my pipe, "my Watson's a damn sight harder to kill than that."

WATSON

The damned sky fell in on me and for a moment all was noise, pain and dust, then blackness as I passed out of consciousness.

The next thing I knew there was a pair of monstrous hands on my lapels, and I was being pulled out of the rubble.

"No," said Kane, "not like that. That would be too easy."

He threw me away from the collapsed ceiling, tossing me to the ground at the far end of the passageway.

My head was spinning and it was so hard to focus, I could feel blood washing the plaster away from my temple and cheek. I was no doubt concussed and would need several stitches. If I was lucky enough to get away with no more wounds that is, something that seemed incredibly unlikely given the attitude of the brute staring down at me.

"Father says we should be ourselves," he said, "feed our animal side." He snarled. "Very well. Run!"

I didn't need telling twice, I got to my feet and, shakily, ran out of what was left of the passage and into the open warehouse.

All around was panic and screaming, some of the animals were cowering, some were running in circles. Not so Kane, Kane was in full control.

"Run, man!" he shouted, the words tapering into a howl like that of a wolf. "I wish to hunt!"

I looked around desperately for a weapon but could see nothing. I ran for the stairs that would lead me up to the main entrance, unknowingly passing right by Carruthers and Wiggins on the other side of the wall as they encouraged Mycroft and his security officers up from the underground entrance.

The stairs were hard going, my legs aching terribly as I forced them to move faster up each flight. Finally I was on the ground floor, and I made straight for the door.

Kane followed me outside, his feet pounding on the road as he chased me down the street. I risked a look over my shoulder and saw he had reverted even further. Dropping forward he was loping along on all fours, tongue lolling from between his teeth as he ran.

"Kill you!" he shouted, his voice even more of a canine howl now.

I ran towards the sound of traffic. As much as I didn't want this thing to harm others I would stand a better chance of dealing with it myself if I could only get into the open.

I emerged close to the Euston Road, Kane at my heels.

"Kill you! Bite you! Suck your bones!" Kane lashed out at me with one of his massive hands and he caught me on the shoulder, sending me tumbling into the gutter.

He rose up and pounded his massive hands on his chest, howling up at the night sky.

I got to my feet, shuffling towards the main road.

"No," he said, "no more run."

He leapt for me and I managed to dart to one side, so he collided with a pair of bicycles chained up against a railing. He roared in frustration as the pedals and spokes dug into him. I kept running towards the main road, aware that I had bought myself maybe a few extra seconds, not much, but possibly enough.

I heard the wrenching of metal behind me, followed by a savage barking sound, and then that gallop of his fists bouncing off the road as he ran on all fours. I was scouring the ground as I ran, desperate to spot something I could use – my eyes alighted on the very thing. A dirty child's ball left in the gutter. And with it a desperate idea!

The Euston Road was always busy with cabs and carts, trucks and coaches, all making their way to and from the station. Stopping at the junction, I turned to face Kane as he charged towards me.

"Kane!" I shouted, in my strongest, most authoritative voice, it was enough to give him pause. "Kane!" I shouted again, loud and firm. He looked at me, head cocked to one side. "Fetch," I told him, tossing the ball over my shoulder and onto the busy road.

With a pitiful howl he chased past me and ran after the ball. That howl turned to a scream as an omnibus bore down on him, and Kane met with the lethal, grinding wheels of progress.

CHALLENGER

I could scarcely comprehend the coldness of Sherlock Holmes, to be told that his friend and colleague was dead, and all he could do was smoke. *Damn the man*, I thought, *he's a cold bloody fish!*

Mann and I fought to pull away the rubble before us, even as we became aware of the sound of Mitchell trying to escape from his locked laboratory.

"Shouldn't we deal with him?" I asked, staring at that chilly damned detective.

"I shouldn't concern yourself," he replied, puffing away on his church warden. "Give him a little more time and he'll have dealt with himself. He said it was a concentrated formula so I can't imagine he will manage to last long before…"

There was a terrible tearing sound from the inside of the laboratory, followed by a wet slap such as might be made by hurling a bucket of tripe at a wall. In a way I suppose that is exactly what it was.

"There we are," said Holmes with a smile. "Problem solved."

More hands were helping with the bricks now as Mycroft and his small force had appeared on the other side.

We could hear the sound of gunshots and I found myself wretched at the thought of those poor creatures being killed. I do not doubt that Fellowes and his men acted out of the public interest but, ultimately, the beasts were blameless. It was their humanity that did for them, not the part of them that was animal. What a terrible bastard Mitchell had been! Aye, him and Moreau before him. When would we humans ever learn? We are not the dominant species in this natural world, and the sooner we stop and realise it, the better we all shall be.

Soon the way was clear again, and we found ourselves face to face with Mycroft and none other than John Watson! He was looking distinctly the worse for wear, but alive for all that.

"I told you," said Holmes, patting the doctor on his arm. "My Watson is hard to kill."

"He seems to try often enough," Watson replied.

"Right then," said Mycroft. "Can we please get all this tidied up? I have a hot toddy I wish to be on the outside of."

MYCROFT

I didn't learn anything from the laboratory. I certainly didn't take any of the chemicals I found there, and certainly will not suggest that Mitchell's work is continued, albeit in a safer, more controlled manner.

And anyone who says differently will be shot as a traitor to the Crown.

MEDICAL NOTES

In my last book, *The Breath of God*, I sought to write something of a love letter to supernatural fiction (using the ultimate fictional rationalist to do so). This time my sights were set on the scientific romance, the escapist fun of deluded scientists, mad professors and the monsters mankind does so like to create.

In doing so I have once more raided the work of others so let me take this opportunity to parade the originals, like a man in the dock admitting to his thefts.

My main crime is of course directed at H.G. Wells' novel *The Island of Doctor Moreau*. First published in 1896, Wells' book is thoroughly discussed here and forms the background of everything you've just read. While the conceit of Moreau having been in the employ of Mycroft Holmes has no more justification than that it was fun and brought his brother easily into the matter, I hope the idea that Edward Prendick, the original story's narrator, might lose his mind through his experiences seems a logical enough extension of the original.

When Wells wrote *The Island of Doctor Moreau* he had a point to make. I have resisted following in his footsteps. *The Army of Dr Moreau* is not a polemic, it's a bit of pulp fun. Though it is somewhat depressing to note that, after so many years, I could still have preached had I wished. As a species we haven't learned our lesson when it comes to the kindly treatment of our fellow creatures. What terrible animals we still are.

The other crimes I wish to take into consideration concern the members of Mycroft's ludicrous think tank.

Professor Challenger is sure to be well known to most Holmes enthusiasts as he was another creation of Sir Arthur Conan Doyle. The aggressive giant lay at the centre of the novel *The Lost World*, that glorious romp of dinosaurs and lost tribes. *The Lost World* has inspired many books and movies, not least of all several direct adaptations. Looser offspring include Steven Spielberg's *Jurassic Park* movies and (a personal favourite) 1969's *The Valley of Gwangi*, where cowboys find their way into an isolated biological pocket in Mexico and come face to face with dinosaurs.

My decision to set the action of this book directly after that of the previous volume means that Challenger has yet to have that adventure, hence his scepticism of Professor Lindenbrook's claim to have found prehistoric animals at the centre of the Earth. Lindenbrook of course comes from Jules Verne's *A Journey to the Centre of the Earth*.

Another scientist who would go on to find strange things beneath the bedrock of our planet is Abner Perry (though, as with Challenger, that adventure lies ahead of him in the chronology of this book). Perry, through the funding of his friend David Innes, would soon invent the "iron mole" and the pair of them burrow their way to adventure in Edgar Rice Burroughs' *At the Earth's Core*, the first of his series of Pellucidar novels. I make no bones about the fact that my version of Perry is played by Peter Cushing, as per the movie from Amicus Studios released in 1976, the year I was born! Cushing is a hero of mine and the film continues to brighten up any grey day I chose to screen it in.

The final member of our team is not played by Peter Cushing, nor Lionel Jeffries (though he could easily have been) but rather Mark Gatiss who's performance as Professor Cavor in the 2010 adaptation of *The First Men in the Moon* (another book by H. G. Wells, of course) pleased this viewer no end.

They were small crimes, a fun nod of the hat to the books and movies that have entertained this silly dreamer for the majority of his life.

Carruthers is also stolen from another book, though this time it's one of my own so the sentence should be negligible. He appears in my novel *The World House* and its sequel *Restoration* and he fitted so well that I couldn't resist having him close to hand once more.

Inspector George Mann is a distinctly unsubtle nod of the trilby to the writer of the same name. I featured the countryside detective in *The Breath of God* and decided he may as well return here as, if nothing else, it will make George smile that he finally gets to have some action.

Everybody else is either the product of my imagination or Doyle's (though I have cheekily referenced a scene from the Basil Rathbone movie, *Sherlock Holmes and The Voice of Terror* and Peter Cook's appearance as Watson's editor in *Without A Clue* because once you start it is so very difficult to stop).

ACKNOWLEDGEMENTS

As always, thanks to everyone at Titan and to all those who have supported these new tales of Baker Street, reviewers, publicists and above all readers. It's an address we never tire of visiting.

I am supported in everything I do by Debra, the woman who reads it first. Time and again she is forced to read books on subjects she has no interest in. If that interest is piqued by the time she gets halfway in then I know I have done my job. I love her very much indeed and couldn't write a word without her.

Mother gets the second taste, once a few edits have crept in. If nothing else this makes her think I'm slightly cleverer than I actually am. Which is never a bad position to be in. Again, her support is quite simply invaluable.

Finally, we must thank the dreamers of another age, Doyle, Wells, Verne, Burroughs... writers who looked at the world through a strange lens indeed, cusping a century with some of the bravest and most thrilling stories ever written, stories that stand proud over a hundred years later and mark them as the giants they were.

I am not worthy, but it is to be hoped that the simple act of trying to be continues to bring me closer.

ABOUT THE AUTHOR

Guy Adams has written over twenty books, ranging from novels such as *The World House* and the *Deadbeat* series to novelisations of Hammer movies and more books about Sherlock Holmes than you could shake a Calabash pipe at. He is also the writer of the comic series *The Engine*, working with artist Jimmy Broxton.

www.guyadamsauthor.com

SHERLOCK HOLMES
THE BREATH OF GOD
Guy Adams

A body is found crushed to death in the London snow. There are no footprints anywhere near it. It is almost as if the man was killed by the air itself.

Sherlock Holmes and Dr Watson travel to Scotland to meet with the one person they have been told can help: Aleister Crowley.

As dark powers encircle them, Holmes' rationalist beliefs begin to be questioned. The unbelievable and unholy are on their trail as they gather a group of the most accomplished occult minds in the country: Doctor John Silence, the so-called "Psychic Doctor"; supernatural investigator Thomas Carnacki; runic expert and demonologist, Julian Karswell...

But will they be enough? As the century draws to a close it seems London is ready to fall and the infernal abyss is growing wide enough to swallow us all.

A brand-new original novel, detailing a thrilling new case for the acclaimed detective Sherlock Holmes.

TITANBOOKS.COM

PROFESSOR MORIARTY
THE HOUND OF THE D'URBERVILLES
Kim Newman

Imagine the twisted evil twins of Holmes and Watson and you have the dangerous duo of Professor James Moriarty—wily, snake-like, fiercely intelligent, terrifyingly unpredictable—and Colonel Sebastian 'Basher' Moran—violent, politically incorrect, debauched. Together they run London crime, owning police and criminals alike. When a certain Irene Adler turns up on their doorstep with a proposition, neither man is able to resist.

PRAISE FOR KIM NEWMAN

"Compulsory reading… glorious" Neil Gaiman

"Newman's prose is a delight" *Time Out*

"A *tour de force* which succeeds brilliantly" *The Times*

TITANBOOKS.COM

ANNO DRACULA
THE BLOODY RED BARON
Kim Newman

It is 1918 and Dracula is commander-in-chief of the armies of Germany and Austria-Hungary. The war of the great powers in Europe is also a war between the living and the dead.

As ever the Diogenes Club is at the heart of British Intelligence and Charles Beauregard and his protegé Edwin Winthrop go head-to-head with the lethal vampire flying machine that is the Bloody Red Baron...

"...stunning follow-up to his inventive alternate-world fantasy, *Anno Dracula.*" *Publishers Weekly*

"Gripping... superbly researched... Newman's rich novel rises above genre... A superior sequel to *Anno Dracula*, itself a benchmark for vampire fiction." *Kirkus Reviews*

"A delicious mixture of wild invention, scholarship, lateral thinking and sly jokes... Unmissable." *Guardian*

"How could World War I be made even grislier? Add vampires, as Newman does with great skill in this sequel to his *Anno Dracula.*" *Booklist*

TITANBOOKS.COM